"I'm sorry I made you lose a client."

He made no reply. He simply stared at her, his expression unchanging, his harsh features seemingly carved in granite.

"What I mean is . . ." She exhaled a slow breath. "I've made a mess of it. I didn't think the plan all the way through to the end. It was supposed to be just another way of forcing you to see me so that I could—"

She broke off with a squeal when she found herself jerked backward. And then she was beneath him.

"You're on my bed, Laken," he said in a husky whisper. He had never called her by her first name before, and the sound of it on his lips was erotic.

"Was it an error in strategy?" he continued. "Or have you decided to switch from terrorist tactics to bribery?"

Staring straight into her wide-open eyes, he ran one hand over her tense body and admitted, "I can be bribed."

WHAT ARE *LOVESWEPT* ROMANCES?

They are stories of true romance and touching emotion. We believe those two very important ingredients are constants in our highly sensual and very believable stories in the LOVESWEPT *line. Our goal is to give you, the reader, stories of consistently high quality that may sometimes make you laugh, sometimes make you cry, but are always fresh and creative and contain many delightful surprises within their pages.*

Most romance fans read an enormous number of books. Those they truly love, they keep. Others may be traded with friends and soon forgotten. We hope that each LOVESWEPT *romance will be a treasure—a "keeper." We will always try to publish*

LOVE STORIES YOU'LL NEVER FORGET
BY AUTHORS YOU'LL ALWAYS REMEMBER

The Editors

Loveswept® 711

STARWALKER

BILLIE
GREEN

BANTAM BOOKS
NEW YORK · TORONTO · LONDON · SYDNEY · AUCKLAND

STARWALKER
A Bantam Book / October 1994

ISBN 0-553-44334-8

Published simultaneously in the United States and Canada

Bantam Books are published by Bantam Books, a division of Bantam Doubleday Dell Publishing Group, Inc. Its trademark, consisting of the words "Bantam Books" and the portrayal of a rooster, is Registered in U.S. Patent and Trademark Office and in other countries. Marca Registrada. Bantam Books, 1540 Broadway, New York, New York 10036.

PRINTED IN THE UNITED STATES OF AMERICA

OPM 0 9 8 7 6 5 4 3 2 1

To C.J. and Mark,
my heroes.

And to Amanda. Daughter.
Assistant.
A friend in need.

ONE

The reception room was sleekly modern, minimal to the point of being anal retentive. Chairs consisted of strips of leather held together by bands of satiny wood. Paintings were nothing more than huge splashes of color against stark white walls. Each of the tall, slender plants deigned to put forth one or two glossy leaves. And although one whole wall was glass, it was tinted so that even the light from the sun was repressed.

Controlled. Impersonal. Designed to impress.

Laken Murphy didn't belong in this room. She was fully aware of the fact and didn't need the inquisitive glances from the secretary across the room to tell her so.

She was wearing her navy go-to-court-and-argue-with-the-judge-about-a-stupid-traffic-ticket suit. Her auburn hair had been bullied, cajoled, and spritzed into a more or less orderly French twist. She wore her best gold earrings and every single one of her lucky gold bracelets, and resting on her lap was the designer knockoff purse her friend Rosemary had given her for Christmas.

Back home, Laken would have looked pretty darned spiffy, but in Chicago, in these sophisticated surroundings, she looked a little bit like the manager of an auto-parts store—which, as a matter of fact, she was—and as out of place as a field lark in the middle of a flock of flamingos.

Laken didn't mind that she didn't fit in. She would have gone to see the Queen of England wearing nothing more than her pink bunny slippers, if she had to. She had a very good reason for being here.

Laken Murphy was a woman with a mission.

The path that led her to this particular spot on the globe was a twisted one. It began in the hills of West Texas, twined briefly through a psychologist's office in Dallas, wandered in confusion back to West Texas, and eventually led her to a small, dusty town in the Texas Panhandle.

DeWitt. Two blocks long with caliche side roads that led, not to more town, but to bare, open country.

Laken had gone there hoping to find a man named Joseph Two Trees. What she found instead was a small, plain headstone in a small, forgotten cemetery. Mr. Two Trees had been dead for almost twenty years.

Working on instinct and pure desperation, Laken had sought out an elderly woman who had been Joseph Two Trees' nearest neighbor and closest friend.

And that was when she discovered that rather than a dead end, DeWitt was simply another twist in the road. Because it was from the old woman that Laken had first heard of Marcus Aurelius Reed.

Anabelle Curtis, a small woman, pink and healthy in her old age, obviously enjoyed Laken's visit and was in no hurry to bring the interview to an end.

"Joseph Two Trees was the best man I ever knew," the woman told Laken, her voice soft with memories. "He would help anybody. Peter, Paul, and all. It didn't matter what he was doing or how he felt. Why, he would have throwed down a sack of gold to carry a hurt dog. That's just the kind of man he was."

With a small sigh, she brushed a wisp of white hair from her brow. "I can't tell you how much I miss that man. Been missing him for twenty years now and I guess I'll miss him till the day I meet him on the other side."

"He sounds like a wonderful person," Laken murmured. "And you say Mr. Two Trees taught his grandson everything he knew before he died?" When Anabelle nodded, Laken leaned closer. "What was he like? The grandson, I mean."

"Marcus." The woman frowned, her eyes distant. "Peculiar boy. Strange, solemn ways. Right from the start, Marcus was different. Happens sometimes. Some people are just born with a kind of otherness. I tried to help him. You know, be like a mother to him, hopin' a woman's softness might balance him out some. But I couldn't." She shook her head. "He never let me get close enough. Oh, he had real good manners, remembering to say 'yes'm, please' and 'no'm, thank you.' But I always had the notion he was standing back from the rest of the world, keeping the boy that was inside him, the real Marcus, away from everybody else."

"A woman's softness," Laken repeated. "What happened to his own mother?"

The answer wasn't immediately forthcoming. As it was with most country-bred people, old-world courtesy was deeply ingrained in Anabelle. So Laken waited patiently while the old woman settled her in one of the ancient porch chairs and went in to fetch iced tea and a plate of gingersnaps. After that, there was some polite talk about the instability of both the weather and the modern world.

"Alicia," Mrs. Curtis said at last. "She was Joseph's daughter, Marcus's mother. I don't know what her Comanche name was. Always just called her Alicia." The old woman fell silent for a moment. "It was a heavy burden, raising her alone. You see, Joseph's wife died in childbirth. He was living in the Comanche settlement—that's about ten miles east of here—and he seen what was happening around him. His people were poor and sick, the young ones turning to alcohol and drugs. Back then, nobody cared. They were the forgotten people. Well, Joseph, he wanted better for Alicia, so he moved into that old farmhouse down the road from here and let her mix with the town kids, dress like them, talk like them. He even let her go to college up north."

Mrs. Curtis took a sip of tea, then dabbed at her mouth with a paper napkin. "That was where she met Alexander Reed. He was a rich man, different from anything she'd ever known, but they were head over heels in love, and after they got married, seemed like they was real happy. Then the baby came. Having that baby did something to Alicia. Her Comanche blood came to the fore and just wouldn't let her rest. I don't know the whole of it, but one day she just up and left. Left everything. Husband, fancy house, fancy clothes. Cars and servants. Said she couldn't raise her son in her husband's world. She brought Marcus back here, moved in with some cousins out to the settlement.

"Alexander followed her, begged her night and day to go back with him. I couldn't say what private things happened between them, I just know he finally gave up on her and went back up north. Then"—she glanced at Laken—"this is the part that struck Joseph in the heart. Soon's Alicia's husband took off, she started pining for him. Seems she wasn't happy living with her kin neither."

"Poor girl," Laken said softly. "Anywhere she went, she was a misfit."

"That's it," Mrs. Curtis said, nodding. "Joseph done what he thought was best for her, but he'd made it so's she didn't fit in nowhere. Her blood was Comanche, but she was raised white. Not fish, or fowl, or good red meat. Of course, he took all the blame for that, just couldn't forgive himself for messing up his daughter's life.

"About a year later Alicia died of pneumonia. Alexander, he was so tore up about it, he didn't say a word against Joseph taking Marcus to raise. I guess Marcus must have been two by then. Joseph, God bless him, he was so set on not making the same mistake he made with Alicia, he went way yonder the other direction in raising his grandson."

"He raised him as a Comanche?"

The old woman nodded. "Every day he made sure that boy knew who he was, or at least who Joseph had in his mind for Marcus to be. They didn't go back to the settlement, but them two spent more time out in open country than they did in their house. Joseph was teaching the boy the old ways, secret things. Teaching him to be strong and tough like his ancestors. He wouldn't allow there was a single part of Marcus that wasn't Comanche."

Laken leaned forward. "What happened to him? To Marcus? Where did he go after his grandfather died?"

"Oh, he left DeWitt 'fore that happened. I guess Marcus would have been about ten when Alexander Reed died in some kind of accident. It was in the mountains over in the Old Country somewheres. Skiing, if I remember right. Then all a sudden, one day this woman shows up in town."

Anabelle shook her head. "I never met a woman with more spite in her eyes. Said she was Alexander's sister and that the boy belonged to her. Not with her, mind. *To* her. She told Joseph right out that she was going to take Marcus. Which she did. It took two years of lawyer fighting, but she finally got custody of the boy."

She drew in a shaky breath, her pale eyes full of sadness. "That boy never cried a drop. He was only twelve years old and they was taking him away from everything he knew and loved, but there was never a tear in his eyes. His face looked like it was carved out of pure, hard rock. I reckon that was his Comanche training coming out. Joseph had taught him good. But I don't mind telling you, it gave me a chill. Just didn't seem natural."

"And Mr. Two Trees? Did he handle the separation in the same way?"

Mrs. Curtis gave a short, rough laugh. "Don't you believe it. Losing that boy's what killed Joseph. I saw him dying a little bit every day. He lasted five years, then just plain gave up the fight."

She made a soft sound of regret. "Marcus didn't even come back for the funeral. I always prayed Joseph didn't know about that, that he wasn't watching from heaven, with his heart breaking because his only grandchild wasn't at his grave to see him buried."

When Mrs. Curtis fell silent again, Laken followed suit, unwilling to intrude on what seemed like grief. A moment later the old woman blinked several times and shook away the sadness, smiling at Laken as she offered her another gingersnap.

"You said Alexander Reed was from up north," Laken said, reaching for a cookie. "Do you remember exactly where that was?"

Mrs. Curtis frowned. "I don't recall that I ever knew . . . hold on, seems like there was something. Something my daughter said. Just set here while I find my box."

A moment later she returned with a cardboard box. "I'm nearly sure my Sara Dan said something about Marcus in one of her letters. . . ."

Her voice trailed off as she sat down and began to sort through the contents of the box.

"Look here," she said a moment later. "Here's a picture of Joseph. Taken back before his troubles started."

The black-and-white photo showed a heavyset man with dark complexion and thick black hair. Even though he wore western clothes—a cowboy hat, boots and jeans, long-sleeved plaid shirt—his broad, Native American features were unmistakable. Laken saw immediately why Mrs. Curtis had loved him. There was a twinkle in those dark eyes that made Laken's lips automatically curve in a smile.

She was still studying the snapshot when her hostess found the letter she had been searching for.

"Sara Dan, she lives up in Kansas City. In this letter she's telling me about how the people she works for are putting up a new office building. Fifty stories." She sent Laken a skeptical look. "I don't trust buildings that high. Just asking for trouble." Turning her attention back to the letter, she said, "Right here she says, 'Guess who designed it, Mama? Henly, Noble, and Reed out of Chicago. I know that doesn't mean anything to you, but listen to this, the Reed part is our Marcus.' Sara Dan and Marcus hung around together some when they was little," Mrs. Curtis added in an aside. "She goes on to tell about how you could have knocked her over with a feather when she saw a letter with his name printed on it. Marcus Aurelius Reed. Let's see . . . yes, here it is.

'From what I hear, the Reeds have been big shots in Chicago since Noah built the Ark.' "

She put the letter down and met Laken's eyes. "Chicago. This here was sent about six years ago, but since his family is dug in there pretty solid, I guess he'd still be there."

Chicago. Laken exhaled a slow breath. The twisted path was going off in a new direction. Please God, let this turn out to be the final one.

Glancing up, she found that Mrs. Curtis was holding out another photograph.

"This is a picture of Marcus, made just before they took him away," the old woman explained.

The boy in the snapshot wasn't dressed in western wear as his grandfather had been. His chest was bare, and he wore faded jeans and soft leather moccasins that were laced tightly around his calves. His black hair fell to his shoulders and was bound by a strip of cloth tied across his forehead. In features and dress, he was Comanche.

It wasn't, however, the outward appearance that so firmly captured Laken's attention. It was the boy himself. There was unconcealed arrogance in the way his shoulders were thrown back, a provoking boldness in the tilt of his strong chin. He had the look of a warrior. Untamed. Unbreakable.

Then, on looking closer, Laken found something that disturbed her more than a little. She knew something about twelve-year-old boys and the look in this one's eyes was wrong. It shouldn't have been there.

The deep-set black eyes of this man-child were those of an injured animal. And Laken knew without a doubt that in the way of an injured animal, those same eyes would turn savage if anyone tried to come too close.

As she sat staring at the snapshot the hair on the back of her neck stood on end and she was shaken by the strangest sensation.

Although she couldn't even begin to understand it, Laken was suddenly convinced that Marcus Aurelius Reed, the man who had once been the arrogant, soul-damaged youth in this photograph, would mark the end of the twisted path.

TWO

So now Laken was in Chicago, sitting in an intentionally imposing room, seeking the help of a man who didn't know her from Adam.

She had flown in the day before, rented a room in a not-so-wonderful part of town, and immediately called the architectural firm of Henly, Noble, and Reed.

Marcus Reed, however, was not an easy man to see. His secretary, the plump, young woman presently sitting across the room from Laken, had spent quite a bit of time trying to get the latter to state her business, which of course Laken couldn't do. Not over the phone and not to a woman who almost certainly would have hung up on her.

Finally, like Ali Baba standing before the cave of thieves, Laken had discovered the magic words. Joseph Two Trees. One mention of his name and all doors opened.

"Mr. Reed will see you now."

Drawing in a deep breath, Laken rose to her feet. She smoothed down her jacket, straightened her shoulders, and walked across the room to the oak door she had been staring at for almost an hour.

On the other side of the door was a large office with the same cutting-edge-modern feel as the reception room except that the furniture was more substantial, more masculine.

An ebony desk, polished to such a shine Laken was tempted to shade her eyes, was situated in the center of the room. Behind it was a black leather chair, the back turned to the room.

After an awkward moment she took one of the chairs positioned before his desk and waited.

Occasionally she heard the rustle of paper from the other side of the chair. The only other sound in the room was Laken's heart beating in her ear, each muted thump measuring the slow seconds that ticked by while she waited.

And then the chair swung slowly around.

Marcus Aurelius Reed, if this was truly he, had strong, angular features and strange, shuttered eyes. Deep set and black as hell. A bottomless pit in a lost cavern.

The arrogance she had seen in his childhood likeness was still there. Oh yes, it was definitely there, in the set of his shoulders as well as the line of his jaw. But that and his tanned complexion seemed to be all that was left of the youth that had arrested Laken's imagination several days earlier.

No pagan prince here. No fierce warrior. Marcus Reed was, quite simply, a modern businessman. And instead of savage, unendurable pain, his dark eyes were filled with what looked like bored cynicism.

"I'm afraid I've forgotten your name," he said by way of greeting.

"Murphy," she supplied. "Laken Murphy."

His lips quirked in a polite smile. With his steepled fingers supporting his chin, he leaned back in the leather chair and met her gaze.

"I'm sorry I don't have more time to give you, Miss Murphy." The words were clipped, perfunctory. "Why don't you start by telling me what you have to do with my grandfather?"

"Not a thing," she admitted without hesitation. "I had never even heard of Mr. Two Trees until a week ago. I used his name because it seemed to be the only way I could get in to see you."

He showed no reaction at all to her confession. He simply glanced at his watch, his chiseled features perfectly controlled. "And why was it so important that you see me? My secretary tells me you have no need for the professional services of Henly, Noble, and Reed."

"No, I'm not building any skyscrapers today." Imitating his own movements, she leaned back in her chair. Avoiding his dark eyes, she ran her gaze over the lines of his face, attempting to see beyond the unreadable surface. "It's more of a personal need," she added after a moment.

This statement brought, at last, a reaction. Raising one brow, he gave her a look that was every bit as assessing as hers had been. But unlike hers, his was an overtly sexual appraisal.

"Oh yes?" he murmured softly.

The attempt to make her self-conscious was so obvious, Laken almost laughed. Almost. Relief was stronger than amusement. At the moment she was extremely grateful this man was giving her only a small part of his attention. She had a feeling that if he were truly interested in unsettling her, he could have done so with very little effort.

"Yes," she said, keeping her voice carefully matter-of-fact. "But I'm afraid it's a little complicated. I need—actually I—you see . . ."

She let the words fade into silence. Scratching her chin with the tip of one pink nail, she considered her next words. She had gone over a dozen times what she intended to say to him, allowing for different reactions and responses on his part. The conversation had gone better in her head.

"Maybe I should tell you about my little brother."

"If you think it's absolutely necessary."

She recognized the dry note of sarcasm in his voice, which was obviously intentional, and although it brought a slight crease to her brow, it didn't stop her. Laken was stubborn. She had ignored stronger hints in her life.

Keeping her gaze on a point just beyond his left shoulder, she began at the beginning: Seven years ago when the brakes failed on a cement truck, sending it through an intersection to broadside a car.

Laken had been eighteen at the time, in her first semester of college, and the unlucky car in the intersection had contained her entire family.

Both her parents had been killed instantly, but by some miracle or accident of fate, the five-year-old child occupying the backseat had survived with nothing more than minor cuts and bruises. Laken had then taken over the job of raising her younger brother.

"C.J. is twelve now," she said, still addressing Marcus Reed's bookshelves. "His real name is Charles Johnson Murphy, but we've always called him C.J. He's not an ordinary child. He's—"

At a loss to explain how special her brother was, Laken began to dig around in her small handbag, an action that caused the gold bracelets on her wrist to jangle like wind chimes in a sudden gust of wind.

"Here's a picture of him," she said as she finally located the snapshot, the one that showed her brother standing next to the project that had won him top honors at the science fair.

Although Marcus Reed accepted the photograph, he barely glanced at it before handing it back to her. "I'm sure he makes you proud."

"More than you can possibly imagine," she said slowly, his colorless tone bringing deeper furrows of confusion to her brow. She had never met anyone so cold and unemotional.

Giving her head a small shake, she picked up her story. She told him a little about raising C.J., watching him grow, and what it was like to be in charge of a twelve-year-old boy with a vivid imagination and awe-inspiring IQ. She told him how, three months earlier, she had taken C.J. on a camping trip to the hills of West Texas.

It was near the end of the four-day trip that her brother had made the discovery.

"C.J. knows things," she said, her gaze shifting from the bookcase to the stone-faced man behind the desk. "All kinds of things. You can't imagine the knowledge that's crammed into that twelve-year-old brain. So when he said the broken pieces of clay were artifacts, I didn't doubt him for a minute."

Laken had informed the park ranger of the discovery; the ranger, in turn, had informed the appropriate authorities.

"We met the archaeological anthropologist who will be working the site—Anson Mathias, a really sweet man—and apparently it was inhabited by a group of Comanche mystics. Wise men. At least that's what Anson believes. Something he heard in an old legend or folktale made him—

Anyway, Anson was hoping the site would prove a pet theory of his, sort of like Schliemann with Troy. You know, turn mythology into history."

"Did it?"

She shrugged. "The jury is still out. By the time Anson got there, our vacation was over. We went back home to Allen." She smiled. "Allen is where we live. It's just north of Dallas, the perfect place to raise children. I can't really explain it. The people are—"

"Miss Murphy."

"Sorry. Anyway, a couple of weeks after our vacation, C.J. was playing basketball with some of his friends and he fell. I know that's not unusual in itself. Twelve-year-old boys are notoriously clumsy. But—" She stopped and swallowed hard. "You see, he kept falling. Then one day he . . . um . . . he—one morning when he got out of bed, his legs wouldn't stop shaking."

Laken's throat closed as she remembered the terror that had gripped her that day, all the wild thoughts that had gone through her mind. There were so many debilitating, even deadly, diseases that struck children. It could have been anything.

When the man behind the desk shifted his position, drawing her attention back to him, she cleared her throat and once again picked up her story.

"His pediatrician was stumped. There was noticeable muscle deterioration, but he couldn't find the cause, not even when he put C.J. in the hospital for tests. Test after test after test. They tested my brother for every disease known to man. Ordinary diseases. Exotic diseases. Diseases that strike only on Friday noon after the third Thursday in June."

When she heard the hoarse frustration in her voice, she paused, exhaling a slow breath as she brushed a stray curl from her forehead.

"It was the resident psychologist who came up with the theory that C.J.'s illness was psychosomatic." She frowned in irritation. "Of course, these people never say anything definite. Could be. Highly likely. A strong possibility. He said my brother's illness could be a manifestation of the guilt he felt for surviving the accident that killed our parents. Although C.J. seemed to have handled the trauma well, the onset of puberty might have brought it all to the surface. He recommended psychiatric therapy."

"But you don't agree with him?"

"What I think isn't important. The point is, C.J. doesn't agree."

Before Marcus Reed could give her a skeptical look, Laken's lips curved in a wry smile.

"You still don't understand about my brother. You're wondering why I didn't just tell him that he's a kid and I'm an adult, so he should keep his mouth shut and let me do what I think is best. Well, that's not the way it works with C.J. He's more intelligent than most adults I know. So when he talks, I make it a point to listen."

"And what did he say?"

"He says the doctors are wrong. He can see how circumstances would lead them to reach the conclusion they did, but in this particular case, it's a false conclusion. He doesn't, however, hold their misdiagnosis against them. You see, they don't have all the facts. And even if they did, 'twentieth-century conceit combined with the exclusionary thinking that is endemic to the American medical establishment' would have blinded them to the truth," she repeated, mimicking her brother's lofty tone.

Marcus Reed raised one dark brow. "Interesting child."

"I told you," she said with unshakable pride in her voice, "he's special."

"I don't suppose he told you what the real diagnosis is?"

Neither his tone nor his expression had changed, but something in his eyes convinced Laken that she had finally caught a fragment of his attention.

"As a matter of fact he did," she said. "He said he feels stupid for not having thought of it sooner. According to C.J., when you put all the facts together and carefully consider the chain of events, you can see that the truth has been there the whole time."

"And the truth is . . . ?"

She shrugged. "The truth is he's a victim of demonic possession."

There followed a long, long silence.

Laken squirmed in her seat. She glanced over Marcus Reed's right shoulder and took in the view. She switched to his left shoulder and revisited the bookshelves, wondering if whoever dusted this room took the books out or simply wiped at the visible bits. She uncrossed her legs and recrossed them, this time with the left knee over the right. She even thought about getting out her emery board and doing her nails, since it looked as if she would have the time.

"Demonic possession," he said slowly, then repeated, "Demonic possession." After a brief pause he cleared his throat. "Yes, of course. I should have thought of that. Let's see . . . I guess I could—we're in the age of specialization, you understand, so normally I refer all cases involving demons to one of my colleagues downtown. Why don't I ask my secretary to get that number for you?"

She settled back in her chair, deciding that on the whole, he had taken it rather well.

"It threw me for a loop too," she said, smiling in understanding.

"No . . . not at all. I'm sure this sort of thing happens all the time."

She swallowed an inappropriate but irresistible bubble of laughter. "No, it doesn't. But I promise you, my brother is completely serious. He believes there is a demon inside him that's making him sick."

He stared at her. "You have witches in Allen, Miss Murphy? A satanic cult? Or maybe the local chapter of Druids International is respon—"

He broke off, his eyes narrowing. "Your brother said it's necessary to put all the facts together. The site he discovered in West Texas—"

The man was acute. She had to give him that. It hadn't taken him long to come up with the right answer.

Laken nodded. "He's convinced he got in the way of some ancient Comanche hex. Sort of like the King Tut thing. C.J. found the site, therefore it's his fault that it's now being profaned by outsiders. In retaliation the spirits of the place put a curse on him—in the form of a little demon—and there is nothing modern medicine can do for him."

"I see." He leaned back in his chair again. "Have any of the archaeologists working the site been stricken with this mysterious ailment?"

"No, but—"

"Then don't you think it's possible the doctors are right?"

"Of course it's possible. In fact, it's the only logical explanation."

Laken hadn't been able to keep the anger out of her voice. She was afraid for her brother. Whatever was afflicting him was real. C.J. was genuinely ill.

Raising her chin, she drew in another slow breath. "But logic also tells me that if the disease is all in my brother's head, the cure must be there as well. If he really believes ancient spirits are causing this thing . . . if his mind is strong enough to make him sick, then his mind should be able to provide the cure as well."

"Isn't that what counseling is supposed to do?"

"I believe in psychiatry," she said, her voice soft as she stared beyond him, out the window into the distance. "I have a friend who used to scrub her hands with steel wool and now—"

She broke off and turned her head to meet his eyes. "It takes *too long.* C.J. is getting weaker every day."

When her voice almost broke on the last words, she dug her nails into the palms of her hands, forcibly rejecting the negative thoughts.

"I've talked to him, made him promise to humor the ignorant doctors and go ahead with therapy. But don't you see?" She leaned forward, her voice growing taut. "I can't simply sit back and turn this over to other people, no matter how much they're supposed to know. For them, for all those experts, this is a medical problem, pure and simple. But for me, it's personal. Damned personal. C.J. is my responsibility. It's my job to keep him safe. No matter what I have to do."

She gave her head a helpless little shake. "I didn't automatically take this route. I talked to dozens of experts in child psychology. I visited every psychic in the phone book. I even convinced a friend of mine, an actor, to dress up like Hollywood's version of an American Indian and dance around C.J.'s bed. And even though it was nice seeing C.J. getting a really good laugh, that was all it accomplished." Her shoulders quirked in a small shrug. "So now I have to try something else."

It was at this point, without understanding how it happened, that Laken lost him. It was obvious that he had been intrigued against his will by parts of her story. But now, in an instant reversal, impatience hardened his features and he glanced again at his watch.

"Miss Murphy, I understand that you're worried about your brother and I don't want to appear unsympathetic, but I'm afraid I have a particularly heavy schedule today. Are we getting anywhere near the part where you explain why you came all the way to Chicago to see me?"

She stared straight into his dark-as-hell eyes. "Anson Mathias knew your grandfather years ago. He said Joseph Two Trees was a Comanche shaman. A medicine man."

He stiffened in an almost imperceptible movement. "So?"

"He said Mr. Two Trees learned his art from his father, who learned it from his father, and so on, all the way back in time. He also said that whenever he questioned your grandfather about the legendary mystics, he always laughed and claimed it was a fairy tale, but something in his eyes convinced Anson that Joseph Two Trees knew more than he was admitting. He believes your grandfather knew the ancient holy ways, the secrets those mystics learned on that hilltop centuries ago." She paused. "And I think he taught those secrets to you."

There was only a slight hardening of his voice when he said, "I repeat, so?"

A moment later his brow creased in a frown as he examined her expression. "Don't tell me you came here for medical advice. Did you really think I could write a prescription for a little Comanche magic?"

"I'm not after advice," she said slowly. "I want you to come back to Texas with me. Don the old loincloth, shake some bones, and cast the evil spirits out of my brother."

If nothing else, this at least startled him out of his boredom. He laughed outright. "You're kidding." A moment later his amusement faded and died under her unswerving gaze. "You're not kidding."

She shook her head. "You're the only one left. It's you or nothing."

"Then it's nothing."

She glanced down at her hands, then back to his face. "I heard a lot about Joseph Two Trees while I was in DeWitt. If he were still alive, he would help me."

He was silent for a long, tense moment. "I am not Joseph Two Trees."

"No," she agreed softly, "more's the pity." Exhaling a slow breath, she added, "But you're all I've got, so you'll have to do."

Although she would have thought it impossible, his midnight eyes became even darker as anger took hold. It was the first strong, genuine emotion she had seen in him. Interesting the way it made his features even more vital, more compelling, more unyieldingly male.

"Evidently I'm not getting through to you." His voice was tight, almost harsh. "I won't 'do' at all."

Almost immediately he brought his anger under control, and as he leaned back in the tall chair, bored cynicism filtered back into those dark eyes.

"You can't really tell me you thought I would fall right in with your plans." His lips twisted in scorn. "Come back to the real world, Miss Murphy. Why in hell should I?"

"You mean, what's in it for you?" She shrugged. "I don't know. I guess I was hoping you might think it was a hoot."

"You were hoping I might think it was a hoot?" he repeated slowly, his head drawn back, his tone incredulous.

"If someone came to me with this proposition, I would do it for kicks." Reading the change in his expression, she added, "Yes, I know you're not me, a fact for which we're both extremely grateful. Let me tell you something. Yesterday I had some time to kill. So I went to the library and checked up on you in back issues of the local newspapers. I don't want to hurt your feelings, Mr. Reed, but from what I saw, your life isn't exactly a giggle a minute."

He stared at her for a moment in silence. "While I appreciate your effort to add excitement to my life," he said slowly, "if ever I feel the need for some 'giggles,' I don't have to go out of town for them. I can find all the entertainment I want right here in Chicago."

He rose smoothly to his feet. "And now I think this meeting is—"

"What's your Comanche name?" she interrupted. Mrs. Curtis hadn't been able to tell her and it was something Laken had been wondering about since she first saw his photograph.

He didn't even pause as he moved around the desk. "He Who Has No Patience with Annoying Redheads from Allen, Texas, Who Jingle Incessantly and Ask Outrageously Impertinent Questions."

"A little tough to get a nickname out of that," she muttered.

"It was a pleasure meeting you, Miss Murphy," he said as he reached the door and opened it.

She followed his movement with her gaze. "Something tells me you're being sarcastic again."

"Trust your instincts. Give my regards to the good folk of Allen."

Rising to her feet, she turned to look at him. Since the moment she had walked in, Marcus Reed had been looking down his arrogant, aquiline nose at her, as though she were some unknown but infinitely inferior form of life.

His attitude hadn't made her angry. There wasn't much that made Laken angry. Things like this, the follies and foibles of her fellowman, always piqued her curiosity.

But now he was dismissing her, as though he expected this to be the end of it.

"I won't be going home just yet." The gold bracelets jangled as she leaned down to pick up her purse. "Chicago's a famous city. I couldn't leave without taking in some of the sights."

"I'm sure there are several excellent bowling alleys."

This time his attempt to put her in her place made her laugh.

"You've got a smart mouth," she said, shaking her head. "I like that in a demigod. Maybe I'll see you around."

"I doubt it."

She glanced up and smiled as she passed by him. "We'll see," she said quietly. "We'll see."

THREE

"What was he like?" Rosemary asked.

Resting the phone on her stomach, Laken leaned back against the simulated-wood headboard and spent a moment considering her friend's question.

"Remember Mrs. Watkins?" she said finally.

"Our old Sunday-school teacher? The one with lavender hair and a nose the size of a small dog? Sure I remember her. Once a month she would ask us over to her house for tea and cake. Stale pound cake and spiced tea made with orange-drink mix and a little bit of cinnamon. Putrid stuff."

"Remember the way she always got palpitations if we touched anything in her house, like we were plague carriers or something. Marcus Reed was more subtle than Mrs. Wat—actually, now that I think of it, he wasn't all that subtle. In fact, he was condescending as hell. But he was better looking than Mrs. Watkins. Sexy as all get out. You might even say—"

"*Lake!*"

"Sorry." She let out a sigh of regret. "The truth is, he was a real butt head."

"I told you he wouldn't do it," Rosemary said in her lazy, doom-is-looming-but-I-can't-be-bothered-to-get-out-of-the-way voice. "And who can blame him? It was an insane idea. You're not only wasting time and putting your job in jeopardy, you're using up all your savings."

Technically speaking, the money in the bank wasn't Laken's savings. It was the insurance money that had come to her after her parents' death.

"That money is for C.J.," she told Rosemary now. "For college. But that's a distant need. This is immediate. Do you understand what I'm saying? Dead children don't go to college."

"Oh, for Pete's sake, you're as bad as he is. He's not going to die. Everyone from the doctors to Mr. Jenkins at the hot link stand has told you that this is all in C.J.'s head. The kid is schizoid. Over the edge. One taco short of a combination plate. Haven't I always said so?"

Laken smiled, picturing the woman who had been her best friend since grade school. Right now she would be slumped down on the couch, her feet propped up on the coffee table, a jumbo bag of potato chips at the ready. Her shining blonde cap of hair would be slightly ruffled, her glasses slipping down on her nose. Rosemary's glasses changed with her mood. One day she would be seen in Elton John rhinestones, the next Benjamin Franklin wires. The ones she wore most often were round and tinted and made her look like a giant bug, the kind that would bite just for the hell of it. She was thin enough and her looks were dramatic enough for her to be a model if she chose. She did not choose. For the past five years she had run a small, successful catering business out of her home.

More recently, however, Rose had been running her business out of Laken's house so she could take care of C.J. while Laken followed the twisted path. Rosemary LaValle was that rare thing, a friend in need.

"You accuse him of being mental only when he gets the better of you in an argument," Laken said.

"Which doesn't happen as often as he thinks it does," the blonde muttered. "You should see him, Lake. He's in there in his bedroom, his arms folded across his chest, his voice deep and mystical as he chants and calmly prepares for death. Talk about melodrama. The little fruit loop is even making me write down instructions for his funeral."

Laken swallowed a sound that was something between a laugh and a sob. "How does he want to be buried?"

"The final decision hasn't been made. He's still running through the list of possibilities. At first, he wanted his body to be laid out on wooden stilts, Indian style, so the vultures could pick his bones. But then he was afraid that would be sacrilegious because he doesn't have any Native American blood." Rosemary paused and Laken could hear the crunch of potato chips before she spoke again. "Of course, if you believe him, there's *something* Native American in him. A little old Comanche demon ought to count for something."

"How did it go today?"

"He seems fine, but you know how he is. Anytime I ask how he feels, he gives me a smart-ass answer, which wouldn't be so bad if he would use words I understand. I always get the feeling there's an insult hidden in there somewhere."

"Let me talk to him."

She heard Rosemary yell for C.J. to pick up the phone in his room and a moment later he came on the line.

"Yo, sis. So how's Chicago?"

"Windy," she said with a laugh. "How's Allen?"

"Not nearly as windy since you left."

She huffed, pretending to be offended by the insult. "I don't talk that much. Okay, maybe I do. But I just happen to have spent a lot of time reflecting on life, and since most people haven't, I feel it's my job to clue them in."

"Isn't it a shame that the people who need you most are the ones who hide behind doors when they see you coming?"

She grinned. The dry note in his voice reminded her of the man she had seen earlier that day. No wonder Marcus Reed's sarcastic attitude hadn't offended her. She was used to it.

"How are you feeling, you obnoxious little pig?"

"Puberty progresses. This morning I found two hairs on my chest. And don't believe Rose when she says it was only pajama fuzz. My pajamas are green."

"I hate to be the one to tell you, but hairy men are out this year. All the real men are getting their chests waxed." She paused, rubbing her chin with one finger. "See any purple martins around the feeder today?"

Although Laken had purposely kept her voice light, they both knew what she was really asking. She wanted to know if her brother had been out of bed today. She wanted to know if the muscle deterioration had finally taken away C.J.'s ability to walk.

"The legs are still wobbly," he told her, cutting through the pretense, "but I'm not worse, so chill out. The status is definitely quo."

"That's good. You know . . . actually that's probably a good sign. If it's stopped progressing, maybe—"

"Cut the crap, Lake. We've been through this

before. It will stay the same for a week or so, then it'll get worse. It always does."

Not this time, she told herself after she hung up the telephone a few minutes later. This time would be different. It had to be. Laken would make sure of it.

Walking to the window, she leaned her forehead against the cool glass.

No one, not even Rosemary, really understood Laken.

"Laken never takes anything seriously," she had heard Rose say more than once. "She doesn't fight against life. She just laughs and thumbs a ride on the winds of change."

That was how all of her friends saw her. No insecurity. No anxiety. No intensity of emotion. And concerning most things, they were right. It didn't pay to worry. Go with the flow was her motto. In the middle of any catastrophe, you could always count on Laken Murphy to be cool, calm, and collected, confident that everything would work out for the best.

But that was before. This time the catastrophe involved her brother.

The motel room suddenly turned airless as fear, like a solid, living thing, swelled around her, jamming up against her, sucking away her courage. She wanted to scream. She wanted to run and hide under the bed. But there was no place to run. No place to hide.

Dear God, she couldn't lose C.J.

"He can't die too," she whispered.

Her breathing had grown shallow and her hands trembled uncontrollably. Leaning against the wall, she used all her strength to drag air into her lungs.

C.J. wasn't going to die, she vowed with fists clenched. Laken wouldn't let him. She would get down on her hands and knees and crawl through hell if that was what it took to make her brother well again.

Pushing away from the wall, she began to pace the narrow room, her thoughts now full of battle plans.

Today, in his high-priced, high-rise office, Marcus Reed thought he had put Laken in her place. He thought he had seen the last of the peculiar woman with the bizarre request.

But Marcus Reed didn't know whom he was dealing with. Not yet.

Marcus closed the door of his town house behind him and slowly walked across the terrace, a drink in his hand.

In the dark, where he couldn't see, all the other senses began to tune in to the world. The distance-muffled night sounds. The softly fragrant night smells. The cool breeze brushing across his face.

When he reached the center of the terrace, Marcus stopped. Leaning his head back, he flexed the tight muscles in his shoulders and neck, trying to ease the tension.

It was a futile attempt, and a moment later he found himself fighting the urge to throw the glass down against the stone tiles, just to hear it break.

He was restless. Tight as a wire. What had gone wrong? The work that in the past had held endless fascination had become routine. He couldn't remember the last time he had been involved in an interesting project. Everything that came across his desk seemed a repetition of the last one.

The hell of it was, they were all his designs. If they were boring, he had made them so. A good architect could make the plans for a gas station exciting.

Dammit, he *was* a good architect. At least, he had been once.

Taking another stiff drink of the whiskey, he began to move around the terrace, his steps tracing the perimeter. Each movement was agitated. Unsettled. A tiger measuring the confines of his cage.

More than his work was being affected. The angry restlessness, the taut dissatisfaction was permeating every area of his life. He had become increasingly short-tempered with his friends and coworkers. It was even filtering into the intimate areas of his life.

Intimate? Not quite, he decided with a grim smile. His personal life wasn't all that personal.

Women were simply another thing on the agenda. Monday dinner with the Joneses. Tuesday start another affair.

Another affair. And another and another and another. And like his designs, the women were becoming indistinguishable from one another.

He drew in a slow, labored breath, thinking of the liaison that had just ended. Bitsy VanMeter Posten. Stupid name, Bitsy. It couldn't possibly refer to her physical appearance. Bitsy was built like a brick outhouse. The nickname was more likely a tribute to her mental acuity.

Swinging around, Marcus swore silently, disgusted with himself.

It wasn't fair of him to take his resentment out on poor Bitsy, even in his thoughts. She was in no way to blame for his restlessness. It had been there before he started seeing her and was still with him now that the affair had ended.

Two days ago Marcus had gone to Bitsy's apartment to tell her, as gently as he knew how, that it was time for them to call it quits.

To say that she hadn't taken it well was an understatement.

There had been immediate, unmistakable fury in the blonde's eyes. But Bitsy was too experienced to give in to her anger. Instead, she began to cry, an affected little tremble in her voice as she told him that he was the love of her life, then accused him of carelessly breaking her innocent heart.

Bitsy's heart. Bitsy's itsy-bitsy heart.

Marcus laughed aloud, and because the darkness made his hearing keener, he couldn't hide from the bitter hardness of the sound.

Bitsy hadn't loved him, had never felt anything even vaguely resembling that gentle emotion for him. From the beginning, their separate motives had been clear. Physical need on his part, avarice on hers. If her heart was truly broken, it was only because Bitsy was going to miss all the money Marcus had spent on her.

In an uncharacteristic flight of fancy, he tried to imagine the kind of marriage he and Bitsy would have had. The fantasy sent an instant icy chill rushing through his veins. No love. No warmth. Not even honesty between them.

They would have stayed together for a couple of years, fighting over extramarital affairs and who said what to whom at which boring party. Then would come the messy divorce and hefty settlement.

As far as Marcus was concerned, he had saved them both a lot of trouble. He had streamlined the process by giving her the settlement now. No muss. No fuss. No divorce lawyer to split the loot with.

The blonde had pretended to be hurt and insulted by the mention of money, but she showed no hesitation in taking his check.

Even though Marcus had briefly desired

Bitsy, he had never loved her. But for one fleeting moment he had found himself wishing that she would reject the check, throw it in his face or tear it to shreds, anything to show that he had been more than a bank account to her.

The idea brought another hard laugh. How stupid could he get? Why should he expect more from a woman than he was capable of giving in return?

As he began pacing again Marcus spent a moment looking back over his adult life, searching his memory to find one person he had truly cared for.

He respected his aunt and uncle and was grateful to them. But they had somehow never fit together as a family. His uncle Philip seemed to be in awe of Marcus. Aunt Miriam wasn't the kind of woman to evoke warm feelings. He supposed they cared about him in their own way, out of a sense of duty, because he bore the family name.

Friends? Yes, Marcus had friends, all successful professionals, interchangeable beings moving in and out of the scene, their presence adding nothing to his life, their absence leaving no void.

And, of course, there were the women. A long line of women. All beautiful. All transient.

The ever-shifting scene was no fault of theirs. There was something missing in Marcus himself. He had learned long ago that desire was the strongest emotion he was capable of feeling. But desire without love didn't last. He had learned that as well. And it was a cold, lonely thing while it did.

Straightening his back, he took another sip of his drink. He was who he was and it was time he came to grips with it. There was no use trying to change his nature. You have to play the hand you're dealt.

Practical advice. Good, solid advice.

But still cold. Still lonely.

Tipping his head back, he gazed at the sky full of stars. A moment later, with no conscious effort on his part, he found himself thinking of the woman who had come to see him today.

Laken Murphy.

He laughed again, but the sound of his laughter had subtly changed. It was softer and this time contained genuine amusement.

Laken Murphy. An original.

He moved across the terrace and sat down in a lounge chair, leaning back as he ran through his encounter with the audacious redhead, a smile playing across his lips. He remembered her husky voice. The little mole just above the right corner of her lips. The way she refused to be intimidated by him. The bold honesty in her eyes. Those extraordinary eyes. Eyes that changed color every time he looked at them. Sometimes blue, sometimes green, sometimes gray. And once when she had been carried away by the intensity of her emotions, they had turned the color of a storm at sea.

Did she know that everything about her, every look, every movement, was provocative?

It surprised him, both then and now, how listening to her, watching her, had affected him. There had been more heat in him then than when he had other women naked in his bed.

Today, in his office, even as Marcus was resenting her for intruding, for reminding him of things he didn't want to remember, he hadn't been able to suppress the strong, unfamiliar sensations she provoked in him.

He had known women more beautiful than she. He had known women more overtly sensual. But none of them had been Laken Murphy.

What would it be like? he began to wonder. What if she were a different person, living here in Chicago, moving in his social circle?

Turning his imagination loose—it seemed to be the night for it—he pictured himself walking into a party with her on his arm. He pictured the way she would look people straight in the eye and speak her mind. No artifice. No social games. Just down-home truth.

The image made him grin wickedly. Aunt Miriam would swallow her tongue.

Carrying the fantasy a step further, he saw himself walking into an imaginary bedroom, her bedroom. She was lying on the bed, her auburn hair making a bold splash of color against the white pillows. She wore—

Here his thoughts paused. What was she wearing? Nothing that was blatantly provocative. And there would be no rows of ruffles and lace.

Emerald-green satin pajamas, he finally decided, with several buttons undone so that the top formed a deep V between firm, smooth breasts. Her eyes—those fantastic eyes—would reflect the green satin and shine with a look of undisguised, unrestrained welcome. For him and him alone.

There would be no games between them, no vying for power. Her eyes said it all. She wanted him and made no attempt to hide her desire. She had no interest in his bank account or his social standing. She wanted only him.

A moment later a sound of contempt caught in his throat. Fairy tales. He, a full-grown, relatively sober man, was sitting in the dark making up fairy tales.

The truth was, if Laken Murphy lived here in Chicago and moved in his circle, she wouldn't be who she was. She would no longer possess the qualities that so intrigued him. The dauntless spirit. The unpretentious honesty. The sincerity in her beautiful, ever-changing eyes.

Besides, he would probably get bored with her in a sustained relationship. Probably.

Giving his head a rueful little shake, he rose

to his feet and began walking toward the back door.

His steps slowed when he noted the curious fact that for a few minutes, while he had sat thinking of Laken Murphy, the taut, angry restlessness had disappeared.

FOUR

Laken sat on the white couch in Marcus Reed's reception room, thumbing through a glossy architectural magazine as she waited.

It had been after midnight when she finally got to bed the night before. She had been too keyed up to sleep. Instead of weakening her, the terror that had momentarily filled the room had renewed her strength. The battle lines were drawn. Fear on one side, Laken on the other. It was a war she had fought before, years earlier when her parents died. Then, as now, she had faced facts and carefully planned what to do next.

Since Marcus Reed wasn't the type to respond to tearful pleas and Laken wasn't the type to beg, she had discarded the idea immediately. Paying him for his time was out because she knew the paintings on his office walls were worth more than her entire stock of earthly possessions. She had even played briefly with the idea of taking her story to the local newspapers, using adverse publicity to force him into going back to Texas with her. Unfortunately most of the world had lost its ability to believe in curses and ancient spirits, so she would likely come across like a lunatic.

Eventually Laken had chosen the only alternative left to her. She would hang in there until she wore down his resistance.

And so here she was. Waiting.

He didn't arrive until almost ten. When he spotted her, he halted midstride and stared.

Laken, who had been watching him from beneath her lashes, waited for the stare to turn into a glare, then she raised her head, nodded in a brief acknowledgment of his presence, and returned her attention to the magazine.

A moment later the door to his inner office slammed shut.

As she let out the breath she had been holding, she felt a measure of satisfaction. He had noticed her.

At the sound of an irate buzz, his secretary, Tess, picked up the telephone receiver. Laken turned her head in that direction, eavesdropping without an ounce of compunction.

"Yes, Mr. Reed," Tess said, her voice meek, her short dark curls barely bouncing at her slight nod. "Yes, Mr. Reed . . . yes . . . no, Mr.

Reed. Yes. Yes, I'll tell her. Without delay. Yes, sir."

Gently replacing the receiver, the secretary sent Laken a sympathetic look. "I'm sorry, Lake," she murmured. "He won't be able to see you today."

Laken smiled. "Don't worry about it, Tess. I already knew he wouldn't see me. I just wanted him to know I was still here."

Casting a wary look toward the connecting door, Tess said, "He definitely knows."

After spending the hour before Marcus's arrival getting to know Teresa Defasio—Tess to her friends—and chatting cozily about the multitude of problems facing the modern working woman, trashing bosses in general and Tess's boss in particular, the two women had formed a bond. Laken knew that the brunette would help in any way she could. The problem was, no one—least of all his secretary of six years—seemed to have any influence over Marcus Aurelius Reed.

At one o'clock, when he came out of his office, heading for a one-thirty luncheon engagement, he walked through the reception room without even glancing in Laken's direction, leaving a little wave of chilliness in his wake.

With an exaggerated shiver, Laken rose to her feet. "I'm going to go grab a burger. Want me to get you something?"

Tess shook her head. "I brought tuna salad from home. Thanks anyway."

So Laken left, but at three, when Marcus returned, she was back on the couch, this time reading a mystery novel she had picked up after lunch. Completely absorbed by the unraveling drama, she didn't even glance up as he passed her.

At six-thirty, when he left for the day, Laken was still on the white couch. A bag of pretzels lay on the cushion beside her and she ate them absentmindedly as she read. She didn't look up as Marcus passed through the room, but the moment the door closed behind him, she quickly closed the book and rose to her feet.

Scooping up her things, she called, "See you tomorrow, Tess," over her shoulder as she left.

When Marcus Reed's silver Jaguar left the parking garage, Laken, in a rented compact car, slipped smoothly in behind him.

As he traveled through the streets of Chicago she stayed close behind. She made no attempt to hide her presence. She wanted Marcus to see her little rented car that was following a few feet behind him. She wanted him to know that she wasn't going to give up.

On Wednesday Marcus sat behind his desk, frowning as he leaned back in the tall leather chair and closed his eyes.

Louis Boujier, the middle-aged heir to the Boujier fortune, was waiting in the outer office. Today they were supposed to go over the proposed changes in the plans for a new Boujier shopping mall.

There was someone else in the outer office. The same person who had been there for the past three days. Marcus was no longer surprised to see Laken when he walked into the reception room. He wasn't surprised, but he was still annoyed.

For three days she had waited in his reception room, eating cookies or little strips of beef jerky, reading paperback novels, or working on crossword puzzles.

And each evening, when he pulled out of the parking garage, he would look in the rearview mirror and see the little compact car sliding in behind him.

Heaven alone knew what she was trying to accomplish. She had made no further attempts to plead her case with him. And she hadn't tried to force her way into his office. She didn't even try to reach him on the phone. She was simply there, intruding on his workday, invading his thoughts.

Laken Murphy was beginning to get on his nerves.

He couldn't believe he had ever fantasized about having an affair with her. Odds were he would have killed her before the first night was over. As a matter of fact, the thought of strangling her was almost as pleasurable as the thought of making love to her had been.

His lips twitched in a wry smile and he silently repeated, *Almost.*

Straightening in his chair, he shook his head and buzzed his secretary to send in Boujier.

When the door opened, Marcus rose to his feet, leaning across the desk to offer the older man his hand. "I apologize for keeping you waiting, Louis. I needed to find some statistics before we start going over the details."

"No apology necessary. I was early."

Louis Boujier, a distinguished-looking ex-playboy, was a self-proclaimed wheeler-dealer. The fact that most of his deals had negative results didn't seem to affect his confidence. He had the Boujier fortune behind him and could afford to fail at an endless number of ventures. The shopping mall was his newest scheme, and on paper it looked good. But given Boujier's record, he would probably screw this up as well.

"Well now," Marcus said as the older man took a seat on the other side of the desk, "why don't we get right to it."

He had barely begun explaining the changes when the older man interrupted him.

"About that sculpture pit," Boujier said, rubbing the side of his nose in a characteristic gesture, "I was wondering if we shouldn't make some changes there."

Marcus's brow furrowed. "I don't understand. You approved Neville's models. I thought you were very enthusiastic about his work."

"I was. I am," the older man assured him.

"If I remember right, it was your idea to offer the public more than a large, enclosed shopping area. According to you, skylights and indoor trees are passé. You wanted Boujier's to be some kind of cultural center. Have you changed your mind?"

"Not at all." He scooted forward in his seat, enthusiasm shining in his eyes. "But something Laken said started me thinking about the sculpture pit."

"Laken?" Marcus repeated slowly.

In the silence that followed, Marcus tried to slow down his escalating pulse rate. Finally, after exhaling a slow breath, he said, "And what words of wisdom did Miss Murphy offer that caused you to change your mind about the work of an artist whose talent has been acclaimed by every expert in the field?"

Oblivious to the tension in Marcus's voice, Boujier smiled. "While I was waiting to see you we started chatting. I told her about the mall and how it will be located in an area populated on the whole by average Americans. Young marrieds with two-point-five children. I explained that the pit would be centrally located, a place for people to pause and take a break from shopping while they absorbed the beauty of Neville's bronze sculpture."

"And?" Marcus prompted.

"And Laken said that while she liked looking

at metal statues as much as the next guy, if she were a mother with two and a half kids in tow, she would appreciate getting them out of her hair for a while a lot more."

"I see." Marcus spent another few seconds attempting to control his blood pressure. "And just exactly what did Miss Murphy want us to replace the sculpture with? Cages? Leg irons?"

This brought an appreciative laugh from Boujier. He shook his head. "She didn't suggest replacing the sculpture, just that its design be altered. Since nothing has been cast yet, that shouldn't be too difficult." His voice was filled with enthusiasm for a new plan. "We have the opportunity of making this an event, something to be experienced, instead of something to be viewed from a distance." Smiling, he waved a careless hand. "It's all perfectly simple. Neville will just have to change the statues so that children can play on them. Laken saw something like that in a magazine. Beautiful but functional."

The older man leaned back with a satisfied smile. "Now. What do you think? How long will it take Neville to come up with something similar for me?"

Marcus eased his gaze away from Boujier, not bothering to hide the fists that were clenched on top of his desk. The man was off in La-La land and wouldn't notice anyway.

How in hell was he supposed to tell the temperamental artist commissioned for the project that he would have to start all over and create something that Fudgsicle-dribbling children could maul and scramble over? Neville was going to blow a gasket.

Glancing back at his client, Marcus said, "I'm sure we can work something out," and managed a stiff smile.

In an equally stiff voice, he led the discussion back to the purpose of their meeting.

Half an hour later, after walking Boujier to the door, Marcus stood and waited until he saw the outer office door close behind the older man, then without turning his head, he said, "Miss Murphy, would you please come into my office? *Forthwith.*"

He ignored the way she repeated, "Forthwith?" several times in a quietly quizzical voice.

Only when she was in his office and he had closed the door did he slowly turn to face her. "What in the name of all that's holy do you think you're doing?"

"Doing?" she repeated in confusion. "You mean out there? I'm crocheting. I admit it doesn't look much like crochet, but that's because it's my first project. I think the discipline might be good for my character."

"From your mouth to God's ear," he muttered. "You know damn well I'm not talking about crochet. I'm talking about your interference in my business. I'm talking about the way you suggested to my client that what I've designed for him isn't what he really needs."

"Oh *that*," she said, her eyes widening in comprehension. "Poor Boojy. He's been rich all his life and doesn't have a clue about ordinary people, who the mall is supposed to serve. I didn't think it would hurt to offer my opinion."

"You didn't think at all." Drawing in a slow breath, Marcus managed to force a degree of composure back into his voice. "This game has gone on long enough. I want you to stay out of my office."

Tilting her head, she studied his face for a moment. "Are you going to call the security guards?" There was not an ounce of apprehensiveness in the words, only curiosity.

"You think I won't?" he said, his voice low, his eyes narrowed.

"I think you won't. If you make a big fuss, people will notice me, maybe start to ask questions. Although it makes me uncomfortable to lie, I can do it for a good cause. I can tell some real whoppers. It might not cause you any permanent damage, but it would probably disrupt your routine for a while. I don't think you'd like that."

His fingers clenched at his sides as he stared down at her. After a moment he said, "I don't react well to threats."

She shrugged. "I'm not all that crazy about them myself, but I do what I have to do."

With frustration tightening every muscle,

Marcus had to put all his effort into regaining control. When he had succeeded, he suddenly noticed her expression.

"What are you doing?" he asked, frowning. "Why are you looking at me like that?"

She shook her head. "When you get mad, your eyes get darker and you stiffen up, but it lasts only a couple of seconds. How do you do it?" Curiosity had changed her eyes to a smoky blue. "I've never met anyone with so much control. It can't be good for you, swallowing your anger like that. If you don't watch out, you'll get ulcers."

He drew his head back in disbelief. "You're amazing. Never, not in all my thirty-seven years, have I encountered anyone like you."

"Thank God," she said with an audacious grin. "You didn't say it but I know you were thinking it."

"If you can read me so well, then you know that right now I'm thinking that if you really wanted to prevent my developing ulcers, you'd *get out of my life.*"

For a moment she simply stood there, her unswerving gaze on his face, her head tilted to the side. Then she moved her shoulders in a delicate shrug and stepped around him to open the door.

"I'll get out of your office," she said quietly. "I'll even get out of your waiting room. But I can't get out of your life. Not yet." Her expression was uncharacteristically sober as she turned her head to meet his eyes. "I have to do this."

And then she walked out.

Gone but not forgotten, he thought testily as he regained his seat behind the desk.

Although Marcus didn't like admitting it, even to himself, he was affected every time her eyes took on that storm-at-sea look. It bothered him to get a glimpse of the intensity of purpose in her.

He genuinely regretted the fact that her brother was ill, whatever the cause. But there was nothing Marcus could do about it. If she had asked for money, if she had asked him to use his influence to contact specialists, he would have done it without giving it a second thought. But what Laken Murphy was asking was impossible.

The Marcus Reed whose help she needed didn't exist anymore.

FIVE

On Saturday, the flow of traffic on Chicago's streets was different from weekdays. Although there were almost as many cars, they were no longer like ants following a predetermined path. Each car struck out on its own.

The neighborhood that was Laken's destination was, by now, familiar to her. She had driven to this resting place of the elite every evening for the past week. Each elegantly subdued town house had its own history. They had been homes to the wealthy since Mrs. O'Leary's infamous cow had kicked over the lantern.

Finally spotting a parking place between a black Fiat and a silver Mercedes, Laken eased in the rented car, hoping the poor compact wouldn't get an inferiority complex. Minutes later she stood on the sidewalk and looked up at the front door of a town house. It was an impressive door, majestic even, the kind of door she would expect Marcus Aurelius Reed to have.

Although she was tempted to use the huge brass knocker, just to hear how it sounded, she settled for the prosaic and rang the bell. While she waited she practiced what she would say to the servant who would answer the door.

But it wasn't a servant who responded to her ring. It was the man himself.

"Oh," she said. The slightly moronic monosyllable wasn't part of her rehearsed speech. It simply came out, as did her next words. "I was hoping you would be a butler." She held up a camera. "I wanted to take a couple of pictures to show Rose and C.J."

Standing in the exact center of the doorway, he made no reply. No greeting. No swearing. No "get the hell out of my face." Nothing.

"Hi," she said, beginning again. "Gorgeous day, isn't it?"

Still no response.

"I happened to be in your part of town, so I thought, what the hey, why don't I stop by and see old Marcus? You don't mind if I call you by your given name, do you?" She paused. "Given name. When you think about it, that sounds a little strange, like someone could take it back if they wanted to."

Not even a twitch of annoyance.

"American Indians have the right idea. I've been reading up on them lately, and if I understand it right, an individual's name is determined by events that pertain to that person alone, something that happened the minute he was born, or something he experienced during his vision quest, or even by some character trait. That makes the name so much more his own." She glanced at him. "Now this is where I pause so you can make a pithy comment that either rejects or confirms my assertion."

No comment, pithy or otherwise.

She ran her gaze over his features. "Hunk of granite, right? Your Comanche name, I mean."

Laken was prepared to stand on his doorstep for the rest of the day if she had to, talking nonsense until she was hoarse and he was shell-shocked. At that moment, however, movement caught her eye. An older man was walking toward them.

"I can't stop thinking about that audit," the newcomer murmured, a frown creasing his smooth brow. "Why after all these years would they decide to audit me now? Not an audit of the company, but me personally. Was it something— I beg your pardon." He had finally spotted Laken and the apology seemed sincere. "I didn't mean to interrupt your conversation."

"You couldn't really call it a conversation." Laken's lips twitched in a wry smile. "I mean, it wasn't an exchange of ideas. I would probably call it a monologue." She caught Marcus's expression from the corner of her eye, and her last word faded away. "Not that it matters," she murmured, shifting from one foot to the other.

From the time she had spent with the back issues of the Chicago newspapers, Laken recognized the older man as Marcus's uncle Philip. Philip Dickenson, owner and chief executive of Dickenson's Clockworks.

As she studied Mr. Dickenson she found she liked his gentle, distracted expression and the subdued sparkle in his blue eyes. The look in those eyes was mischievous, but his hands twitched nervously, as though he were meant to be jolly but had somehow gotten off track.

Stepping past Marcus, she offered his uncle her hand. "I'm Laken Murphy, and I'm sorry you're having a worrisome time."

The older man frowned. "I don't know how I could have gotten to this age without the Internal Revenue people noticing me." A confiding smile curved his lips. "I don't mind saying I'm terrified, Miss Murphy."

"Call me Laken," she said, returning his smile. "I know what you're feeling. I've been audited, a number of times as a matter of fact. The first thing you have to remember is never show fear. From a distance it looks like guilt. The second thing is, holding your breath until you turn blue hardly ever works."

He chuckled. "But you've found something that does work?"

"It worked for me. You see, once your Social

Security number is flagged, they keep calling you in. That is, unless you do something drastic to break the cycle."

Marcus made a slight sound of contempt, the first sound he had made since he opened the door. "I'm sure my uncle appreciates your concern," he said, "but he has a squad of perfectly adequate accountants and tax attorneys who will take care of this problem for him."

Once more he was trying to put her in her place. When was he going to learn that her place was something she would decide for herself?

"I'd like to hear what Laken has to say," Philip said, glancing from Marcus to Laken. "I don't like the idea of going through this again next year. Just exactly how do I break this cycle you referred to?"

"Simple," she said with a little shrug. "You bore them to death."

Marcus rolled his eyes. His uncle, a more discreet man, coughed then said, "I beg your pardon?"

"Be totally honest . . . at length," she explained. "This is, of course, assuming you have nothing to hide. You take in everything you can scrape together. Receipts, record books, snapshots taken on business trips. Give in-depth, drawn-out explanations of everything. Tell them just exactly why the Home for Retired Corporate Raiders is your favorite charity."

"You actually did this?" the older man asked.

She grinned. "Last time I was audited, which was two years ago. I took in four cardboard cartons of records, including receipts written on gum wrappers and affidavits from each of the thirty-seven people who attended my Lottie Moon fund-raising barbecue."

Philip laughed outright. "I love it. I really love it. And by George, I'm going to try it. Even if it doesn't work, it will be worth it to see the look on my head accountant's face when I tell him what I want him to do." He paused, smiling at her. "My dear, you're a breath of fresh air. Are you staying for lunch?"

She glanced up at Marcus. As usual, his expression was closed, unreadable. She couldn't tell what he was thinking, but she was pretty sure it wasn't anything along the lines of "Bravo" or "Way to go, Laken."

"I don't think so," she said to Philip. "I can't just drop in for lunch. It's not polite."

"Nonsense. There's plenty of food. It's just a matter of telling Biddy to set another plate. Isn't that right, Marcus?"

His query brought one of those pregnant pauses she'd always read about. After a small struggle, the silence finally gave birth.

"Why don't you join us for lunch, Miss Murphy?" Marcus asked slowly.

Laken had never heard an invitation laced with so much derision.

Philip, who seemed to be oblivious to the

overtones, smiled in satisfaction. "Call her Laken," he said to his nephew, then to Laken, "We're eating on the terrace today. I can't wait for you to see the back of this place. It's full of horticultural surprises. Do you garden, my dear?"

Glancing away from the cynical amusement in Marcus's dark eyes, Laken said, "I can use a lawn mower and my azaleas are nice enough to make the woman next door despise me, but that's about it."

"Azaleas," the older man repeated with a sigh. "There's something so soft and southern about them."

"I'm from Texas, and for some reason that's not southern. I don't know why, because if you look at a map, it's more south than what everyone calls the Deep South. But you get everybody's back up unless you call us southwestern."

"I'll remember that," Philip said.

Taking her arm, he led her down the hall and into a wide living room. No ultramodern furniture here. The room was filled with antiques. But somehow, it had the same restrained quality as Marcus's office. There was a place for everything and everything was in its place.

From there they walked through the French doors at the back of the room and out onto the terrace.

In Laken's experience, backyards were square pieces of lawn with some trees and flower beds scattered around. Families with children had swing sets and tree houses while the more affluent had swimming pools and built-in barbecue pits.

This was different. It wasn't a yard at all. The long narrow stone terrace was raised and overlooked a small walled area. A walkway, paved with matching stone, twined around carefully tended banks of growing things.

It was the same as inside, she realized. There wasn't a twig out of place. No leaves going brown, no flowers losing their petals, no branch spreading where it wasn't supposed to spread.

At the other end of the terrace, a tall woman with beautifully coiffed silver hair was arranging fruit in a crystal bowl that sat at the center of a small, linen-covered table.

Laken gave a silent whistle of appreciation. The only tablecloth she owned was bright red and saw the light of day only at Christmas, at which time it was always decorated with the same centerpiece, four white candles surrounded by fake holly.

The country mouse, come to town.

"Miriam, my dear," Philip said, addressing the woman with silver hair, "I'd like to present Laken Murphy, a friend of Marcus. Laken, this is my wife, Miriam."

Having never been presented, Laken felt as though she should curtsy or something. Resisting the impulse, she offered her hand instead, which the woman took after a perceptible pause.

Philip's wife, Marcus's aunt, was not a comfortable woman. The set of her lips and the sternness in her ice-blue eyes seemed to have been designed for intimidation.

After murmuring an inaudible but possibly polite greeting, she directed her gaze toward her husband, instantly extinguishing the twinkle in his eyes.

Laken frowned, remembering Amabelle Curtis's summation of Marcus' aunt. *I never met a woman with more spite in her eyes.* She could see why Philip Dickenson had strayed from the path of merriment.

"I thought I knew all of Marcus's friends," Miriam was saying now. "Have you known him long?"

"No, not long."

"That accent," she said, her voice reflective. "You're not from Chicago."

"No, ma'am. I'm from Allen, Texas."

Miriam stiffened. Either Laken's accent was getting on her nerves or she had something against Allen.

"You're in town on business?"

"No, it's personal." Laken glanced at Marcus. "As a matter of fact, I came here to see your nephew."

Judging by her expression, Miriam didn't like the explanation any more than she liked Laken's accent. But then Laken had a feeling there wasn't much Miriam did like.

"And what do you do in Allen, Texas, Miss Murphy?"

The two men seemed to find nothing unusual in Miriam's interrogation. Was this kind of grilling what passed for polite conversation in Chicago?

"I manage an auto-parts store," Laken said finally. "The largest auto-parts store in Allen."

"Impressive." Although Miriam's expression remained impassive, her tone was scornful.

Meeting the older woman's eyes, Laken said, "What do you do in Chicago, Mrs. Dickenson?"

Miriam stiffened. Apparently the questions were supposed to go one way.

"The Dickensons have been manufacturing clocks since the Revolutionary War," she said, her voice cold. "Philip not only owns the company, he runs it, as well as serving on the board of several major corporations."

Laken glanced at Philip and smiled, then turned her attention back to his wife. "I'm sorry. I didn't make myself clear. What do *you* do, Mrs. Dickenson?"

Marcus cleared his throat, Philip coughed, and Miriam's elegant nostril's flared. "Lunch has been ready for the past fifteen minutes," she said. "Why don't we sit down and let Mrs. Bidwell serve?"

During their conversation, someone had moved quietly and efficiently behind the scenes. There was now a fourth setting at the table.

As hostess, Miriam picked up her soup spoon, signaling the rest of them to begin.

"I've just remembered some Texas Murphys," the older woman said after a moment. "They have an estate just outside Houston. Charles and Evelyn." She pronounced it *Eve*-lyn. "Maybe you're related, Miss Murphy. She was formerly Evelyn Radley Hampton. One of the Connecticut Hamptons. Charles is the eldest grandson of Clarence Keynes who founded the Keynes Institute. As well as their place in Texas, Charles and Evelyn also have homes in Friuli-Venezia Giulia and on the Garonne River in France. They recently hosted the Adventures in Art Ball."

She paused, shaking her head in regret. "Poor Evelyn. She detests her husband's family name and for a while considered hyphenating it with her own. Hampton-Murphy. She gave up the idea when she realized it might sound pretentious. Of course, I assured her that where she and Charles were concerned, people don't even notice the common-sounding name."

She sent an expectant look in Laken's direction, who at the moment was a little dazed from information overload. Having no idea how she was supposed to respond, she glanced at Marcus.

You asked for it.

He hadn't said the words, but he might as well have. The satisfied look in his eyes told her he was enjoying seeing her take a position behind the eight ball.

When the silence drew out, Laken smiled and, in desperation, said, "Nice soup."

A sound of exasperation came from the older woman. "Come now, Miss Murphy, are you or are you not related to Charles and Evelyn?"

"Not," Laken said. "My mother was Carrie Louise Murphy. My father, John Thomas Murphy—of the Uncertain, Texas, Murphys—was second cousin to Sean Murphy who took first place at the tractor pull held at the county fair. We had only the one house, unless you count the time we rented a cabin at Lake Texoma for the summer. The only thing my parents ever hosted were picnics and covered-dish dinners. If my mother hyphenated her name it would have been Bigg-Murphy, which would have been a good description of my father since he was six-four, but it wasn't necessary because it would never occur to anyone we know to think Murphy was a common-sounding name, and to tell you the truth, I'm glad I'm not related to people who do."

"Well, really," Miriam gasped, her smooth complexion turning a delicate pink. "I don't know what kind of manners they teach in Allen, Texas, but—"

"My parents taught me that manners are mostly about kindness, about making a guest, even an unexpected one, feel welcome," she said quietly.

Philip gave a startled laugh, which he quickly turned into another cough.

He wasn't quick enough. Miriam turned her head to glare at him. "For heaven's sake, Philip, you know how much that cough irritates me. Besides, isn't there enough noise with Miss Murphy's interminable jangling?"

With a regretful glance at the excellent soup that she apparently wasn't going to be allowed to finish, Laken put down her spoon.

"Do my bracelets bother you?" she asked the older woman. "I've had them so long, I don't notice. I don't always wear them. Only when I need luck."

Which at the moment, I happen to need a lot of, she added silently.

"Why are they lucky?" This was from Philip.

"Different reasons." She extended her arm toward him and pulled a thick gold bangle down to her wrist. "This one is lucky because it was a surprise. I bought an old trunk and found this stuck in the lining. Serendipity." She separated another one. "This one, a teacher gave me for helping watch her son one summer. I had her for English the next year and made straight A's. These two, the charm bracelet and the one with the little bells, my parents gave to me for no special reason." Her voice grew soft with memories. "They came from love and love is always lucky."

After a moment of silence, Marcus said, "Who gave you the last one?"

"No one. I bought it myself."

"What makes it lucky?"

"I was wearing it the time I didn't fall off the roof," she said, her voice distracted.

After carefully ignoring her, he had suddenly turned all his attention to her. She should have been gratified, but something in the look made her more than a little nervous.

Somehow she managed to get through the rest of lunch, then, taking her coffee with her, she walked away from the trio to explore the small back garden. She was looking down at a small, tile-lined pool when Marcus joined her.

"I'm sure nothing here can compare to what you have in Allen."

She glanced up at him. "My backyard has two trees, a little grass, and a lot of bare spots," she told him. "This is nice. Your house, at least the parts I saw, is nice too."

"Nice," he repeated with a rueful smile. "Damned with faint praise. What have you got against my home?"

"Home?" She frowned. "I guess that's it. It doesn't feel like a home. There's nothing of you here."

Her explanation caused one dark brow to shoot up. "You know nothing about me. For all you know, I put my heart and soul into decorating this place."

She shook her head. "No, I don't think so."

"Why not?"

"It's simple. If this house was in any way a reflection of your soul, I would pity you." She smiled. "And when I look at you, I definitely don't feel pity."

Although Laken thought it was an innocent enough comment, the air between them was suddenly electric. Something in him, in the way he was looking at her, had changed.

Moving a step closer, he dipped his head slightly and their eyes met. As the silence between them drew out, the electricity became more intense. The sound of her breathing and her racing pulse seemed loud to her own ears, making her wonder if he could hear them as well.

"What . . ." he began, his voice low and husky.

Although she glanced at him expectantly, he didn't finish the question. He simply let it die away.

"What what?" She moistened her lips then cleared her throat. "I mean, what were you going to say?"

"It wasn't important," he said, giving his head a sharp shake.

The electricity was gone as quickly as it had appeared. His voice was normal again, his tone detached.

"I suppose you know that you've thoroughly charmed my uncle," he said out of the blue. "But then he's a man who's easily charmed. I hope you don't cherish the notion that you'll eventually have the same effect on me, because if that was what you had in mind when you came here today, I have to tell you it didn't work."

Laken shook her head in a gentle reprimand. "You're way off base. The object wasn't to charm you. I had it in mind to irritate the hell out of you." Her lips curving in a grin, she glanced up at him. "And it seems to me it worked just fine."

At first he showed no reaction to her confession, then after a moment he shook his head and laughed.

Laken stared openly. He was actually laughing. The sound fascinated her. The look in his eyes fascinated her. She had begun to suspect he didn't know how to laugh.

"You've been irritating me since the moment you first walked into my office," he said, still chuckling. "So where does that get us?"

She shrugged. "I think we've established the fact that you're not going to help me out of the goodness of your heart. I'm hoping that eventually you'll give in simply to get rid of me."

He sighed in mock regret. "I'm afraid your plan is doomed to failure. My ability to ignore is almost as great as yours to annoy." He paused, frowning. "I suppose following me home every night is just another of your attempts to 'irritate the hell' out of me?"

"The first three times were to irritate you. The last time was to tell you that you had a Big Mac wrapper caught in the door of your Jag," she said, her voice bland.

This time his laughter came quicker and sounded easier, as though he were becoming used to being amused by her.

A moment later Miriam appeared beside them. Her face was stiff, her eyes openly hostile, as though her nephew's laughter had somehow annoyed her.

"Your uncle wants to talk to you," she said, speaking to Marcus while looking at Laken.

After raising a questioning brow—apparently Miriam's tone bothered him as well—Marcus excused himself and walked away.

The older woman gave him a few seconds to get out of range of their voices then stepped closer. "Why are you here?" she asked tightly, no longer making a pretense at politeness. "You said you came to Chicago to see Marcus. Then you barged in today without an invitation, when it was perfectly clear that you weren't wanted. There has to be a reason. What are you up to?"

Laken examined the enmity in Miriam's blue eyes. "It's not really any of your business, but as a matter of fact I don't mind your knowing. I have a problem that I'm hoping Marcus will be able to solve. I need him to come back to Texas with me and use the secrets Joseph Two Trees taught—"

"*You're out of your mind.*" The older woman's voice was shaking with anger. "Do you really think my nephew is going to disrupt his life to go traipsing all over the country to help someone like you? A . . . a *nobody* who gives covered-dish dinners and sells spark plugs to farmers?"

At that moment, without knowing why, Laken glanced up and saw that Marcus hadn't left after all. Although a lush clump of foliage hid him from his aunt's view, he was not six feet away from them, close enough to have heard every word.

He showed no reaction at all to his aunt's attack. His expression was once more a closed book.

Laken raised her chin. She didn't care what he thought. She didn't care if he was secretly applauding his aunt. She didn't care if the whole state of Illinois thought she was pushy and ill-bred. She was not going to give up until she had done what she set out to do.

Marcus stood in the front hall, a bemused smile curving his lips. Minutes earlier Laken had left, the devil once more showing in those incredible eyes as she thanked him for lunch, assuring him that she would see him around. She had been poking fun at him, laughing at him, and she had made no attempt to hide it.

"We'll be going now," his aunt said as she and Philip joined Marcus in the hall.

The older man paused beside Marcus. "I'm glad your friend dropped by. I like her very much, Marcus. She has a way of—"

"*Philip!* Go wait in the car."

Marcus's uncle reacted with a slight shake of his head, then exhaled a regretful sigh before following his wife's orders.

As soon as the door closed behind him, Miriam turned to Marcus. "Your uncle is getting senile. I don't know how he could say he liked that young woman. You know that I've always considered snobbery an abomination, but sometimes, when the difference in people is so outstanding, it would be the worst sort of fakery to ignore it. I know that you can't blame people for the kind of family they were born into, but if there is anything solid to them, they manage to rise above their background. That has not happened with Miss Murphy. She has obviously made no effort to better herself. Everything about her is brash and reeks of the lower classes. The way she talks, the way she dresses, even the way she has the temerity to look you straight in the eye while she's making rude comments."

Marcus ran a hand across his face, hiding the smile brought by his aunt's diatribe. "I don't know, Aunt Miriam. It seems to me that if you're going to make rude comments, it's better to be bold about it. You have to admit, there was no slyness or subterfuge about her."

"You almost sound as though you admire her." Miriam's eyes widened in disbelief. "Don't tell me you're actually considering helping that . . . that person?"

The faint quiver of fear in her voice made Marcus frown. She was genuinely upset.

"No, of course not," he assured her after a moment. "I simply see no need to make heavy weather out of this."

"Promise me you won't go to Texas," Miriam said, her voice laden with intensity and worry. "It would bring back too many memories for you. When I think of how hard I worked to wipe out all those years you spent with your grandfather . . ." She pressed one hand to her heart and met his eyes. "Remember, Marcus? Remember how you were when you first came to us? Little better than a savage. It was years before you acted like a normal little boy."

Having known his aunt for most of his life, Marcus recognized her attempt at emotional blackmail. The truth was, her idea of how "a normal little boy" acted included coping with an army of private tutors, obeying a long list of strict rules, and being exiled to the back wing of the Dickenson mansion. To do her justice, she had done what she thought was best. She was what she was.

"You don't have to remind me of what I owe you, Aunt Miriam. If nothing else, you made it possible for me to function in the real world."

She sniffed. "Well, I'm certainly glad you're aware of that." She cut her eyes toward him. "I want you to swear to me that you'll get rid of that pesky girl as soon as possible. We both know you can do it."

Marcus stiffened. "You should know me well enough to know I don't let anyone dictate what I do," he said tightly. "Not you. Not Laken Murphy. You'll simply have to trust me to handle this situation as I see fit."

His aunt spent another ten minutes wheedling and nagging before she finally understood that he would not bow to her wishes.

Closing the door behind her, Marcus stood for a moment in the hall. Suddenly he began to chuckle. He was recalling the look on his aunt's face when his uninvited guest had asked, "But what do *you* do?"

Laken Murphy might be an irritating thorn in his side, but he had to admit this was the most entertaining visit he had had with his aunt and uncle in years.

SIX

"He's so stubborn," Tess said.

It was Monday. Marcus had an early-morning appointment and wasn't due for another hour.

Laken, who was perched on the side of the secretary's desk, leaned over to take another chocolate doughnut from the box sitting in the middle of the desk.

"I know, as my boss, he deserves my loyalty," Tess continued, "and when it concerns business, you won't find anyone more loyal than I am."

"Hey, you don't have to convince me. The first time I talked to you I knew you were a good secretary."

"But he's cold, Lake." She paused, glancing over her shoulder to make sure her boss hadn't somehow sneaked past her. "Know what they call him? Not just the peons like me, but the other architects too. They call him the Iceman. He just broke off another affair and the poor woman calls two or three times a day, begging me to put her through to him. But do you think His Majesty will talk to her? Not on your life. I have to tell her that he's out or in conference. I'm telling you, the pain in her voice is enough to break your heart."

Frowning, she picked up a doughnut, the last one with sprinkles. "I wish I had the nerve to tell her that she's wasting her time. With him, when it's over, it's over. Finis. So long, Mama."

Laken licked chocolate off her fingers. "Does he have a lot of affairs?"

The other woman rolled her eyes. "You wouldn't believe the supposedly intelligent women who've fallen for him. And not one of them managed to hold on to him for more than three or four months."

The information didn't surprise Laken. She had too often seen the cynicism in those dark eyes. It would take an exceptional woman to hold his interest.

Glancing at the brunette, she said, "Has he ever put the make on you?"

"Laken!" Tess squealed, a blush adding vivid color to her cheeks. "Of course not. He's never even looked at me that way." She frowned. "I'm not sure he even knows I'm a woman."

Whistling a little tune under her breath, Laken glanced away then back again, one brow arched.

"What?" Tess said with a small laugh. "Why are you looking at me like that?"

"Oh nothing. It's just that your voice was a tiny bit peevish when you said he didn't know you were a woman. And I notice you didn't say you would never have an affair with him, just that he would never ask."

The brunette turned even redder and began sputtering an incoherent denial.

Holding up one hand, Laken laughed. "You don't have to be embarrassed. I'm not blind. The man definitely has something. He's not male-model pretty, but there's something about the hard lines of his face and those deep-as-hell, I-hold-the-mysteries-of-the-world eyes. One of those dark, brooding types women are always swooning over."

"But not you?" Tess asked, her tone openly mocking.

Laken grinned. "Well, I wouldn't swoon. Anyway, I never could see Heathcliff as a hero. All the way through the book, I wanted to smack him."

She slid off the desk. "Besides, whether or not I find your boss attractive is academic. I'm in the same category you are. He doesn't see me as a woman." She smiled. "More like a rock in his shoe. And even if he did, he wouldn't have to work too hard to resist my charms. As far as the Iceman is concerned, I'm part of the great unwashed, not fit to touch the hem of his garment."

"I don't know," Tess said. "There's something in his eyes when he looks at you. Something I've never seen before."

"That's possible," Laken admitted. "It's probably a vision of my slow, painful death."

"Lake," Tess began, sounding very serious, "I don't want you to think I'm trying to get rid of you. This job has been more interesting in the past week than it's been in the six years I've worked here. But the thing is, I don't want to see you disappointed, and I'm afraid that's what's going to happen. I don't think you'll ever get him to help you."

Laken studied the brunette's worried features for a moment then exhaled a short breath of frustration. "I don't understand why it's such a big deal. It would take one day. Twenty-four hours. Then he's back here and I'm out of his life. He can forget I even exist."

Moving away from the desk, she walked to the window and looked down over the streets of Chicago. She rubbed one temple with her fingertip as she fought against being influenced by Tess's pessimism. She couldn't even think of failure. C.J. was counting on her. She had to convince Marcus to help her. Anything else was unacceptable.

"Maybe the therapy will work," Tess said, breaking into the silence that had fallen between them.

"I can't count on it, not when C.J. doesn't believe it will work." Laken looked at Tess over her shoulder. "If you think your boss is stubborn, you should meet my brother. Counseling won't work if he doesn't let it. Maybe, in time, someone could convince him that this is a psychological problem, but we don't have time. C.J. doesn't have the time."

She swung around on her heel, her features set. "I'll go back to the town house. Tonight. I'll force my way in and I won't let him rest until he agrees to help me." She raised her chin. "He thinks I've been a pain in the butt this week, but he hasn't seen anything yet."

"You can't do it tonight, not unless you go late. He has a dinner engagement."

"A date?" she asked, her interest caught. "He has a new woman already?"

Tess shook her head. "No, it's business. Prospective clients. You should see the couple he'll be wining and dining tonight. Gaylord and Regina Jameson. They make that couple in *American Gothic* look like party animals."

Scratching her chin, Laken gave the information careful thought. "They're straitlaced?"

"More puritanical then the Puritans. They think color photographs are degenerate." She cocked her head. "You have a funny look in your eyes." She paused, frowning. "You're up to something. What are you planning?"

"I don't know yet. I have to give it some more thought." She glanced sideways at the brunette. "Your lipstick needs retouching."

Tess ran the tip of her tongue over her lips. "I don't wear lipstick."

"Okay, then your nose is shiny."

Tess squinted her eyes and drew her head back in confusion. "My nose is—"

"Tess, you need to go to the powder room," Laken said, emphasizing each word. "That way if some unauthorized outsider should happen to look at the appointment book on your desk, it wouldn't be your fault. Get it?"

The brunette's lips formed a silent *oh*. Rising to her feet, she started toward the door, then stopped and looked back. "You're going to do something evil, aren't you?"

Laken smiled. "I'm going to damn well try."

"I have to be sure you fully understand my intentions. I won't have one of those grotesque glass-and-cement towers that you see all over the country. My building should appear to be a continuation of history. The Jamesons have been in banking for over a hundred years, and I want this structure to reflect that tradition. Tradition, that's the word. I want Jamesons' headquarters to be something my grandfather would have been proud of. I want you to look on this undertaking as a sacred trust. You, as my architect, will have to . . ."

The voice droned on and on. Marcus nodded where a nod was indicated. Mostly he kept silent, eating his meal without tasting it, trying to get through the evening as quickly as possible.

This was the part of being an architect he hated most. Pretending every client knew more about architecture than he did. Pretending every client's opinion—no matter how asinine—was unique, wonderful, and of supreme importance. Pretending he actually gave a damn.

When the waiter finally arrived with dessert and coffee, when Jameson actually stopped speaking to concentrate on a bland-looking pudding, Marcus exhaled a hidden sigh of relief and glanced around the dining room.

Dim lights, elegant table settings, polished people.

After nodding to a couple he recognized from the yacht club, he frowned and took another sip of coffee. The restaurant and the people in it looked the same as always, but for some reason, the sight of it increased his frustration.

At times like this Marcus almost wished he hadn't stepped into his father's shoes at Henly, Noble, and Reed. What would it be like to associate with the up-and-comers, the men and women of his own generation, men and women who were struggling to make their reputations in the field?

Maybe that was what was wrong. Maybe the reason Marcus found no pleasure in his success was because it was none of his doing. Success was simply something else he had inherited from his father.

But there was no use whining about it. Even if he wanted to, he couldn't have changed anything. He couldn't be anyone other than who he was. The Reed name came with guarantees as well as obligations.

Across the room, a woman caught his attention. There was something about her. And then he realized it was her hair. Although her hair was short and sleek, the color was very similar to Laken's.

Marcus shifted in his chair, wondering again why she hadn't been in his reception room today. Had she finally given up and gone home?

Instantly a smile twitched at his lips. No, she hadn't gone home. Although he had known her for little more than a week, already he knew that much about her. Laken Murphy didn't give up so easily.

Then why hadn't she been there?

She didn't know anyone in Chicago. What if she had taken ill?

Then another possibility occurred to him. What if she had wandered into the wrong part of town? She could be in the hospital right now. Or worse. She could be—

Marcus ruthlessly shut off the thought and pulled himself up straighter. Damn her. Even when she wasn't sitting on his doorstep, she still managed to rattle him. It was stupid to worry about her. If she had run into a mugger, Marcus's sympathies went to the thief.

As he continued to berate himself and her, his concentration was broken by a wave of whispers that spread quickly across the room. Glancing up, he saw that the people around him were all staring toward the entrance.

Turning in his seat, he saw that a woman stood in the entrance beside the maître d'. But not just any woman.

Laken.

His eyes widened when he took in her appearance. She wore a dress that would stop traffic. Black and impossibly short, it fit her body like a second layer of skin. The neckline dipped low, exposing the tops of smooth, round breasts. It was a scandalous dress, and most scandalous of all were the heart-shaped cutouts circling her waist.

Swallowing a sound that combined outrage and laughter, he pulled his gaze away from the smooth, creamy flesh of her waistline and examined her hair, which was a wild mass of auburn curls that glinted like polished bronze in the subdued lighting.

It was the first time he had seen her with her hair down. Did she always look that . . . wild when she wore it loose?

Her face was different as well. She usually wore a brownish-pink lipstick, but tonight it was red. Really red. Outrageously, sensationally red.

As Marcus watched she spotted him. She

raised a hand to wave, an action that caused everyone in the room to shift their attention to him.

Marcus ground his teeth and kept his narrow-eyed gaze on Laken, blocking out the others in the room. She leaned closer to the maître d', one hand on his arm, and whispered something in his ear. When she walked away, the normally composed man looked as though he had been hit by a train.

Marcus rose to his feet, determined to head her off, and intercepted her when she was still several feet from the table. Grasping her upper arm, he dug his fingers into the soft flesh. "What in hell do you think you're doing?" he asked in a tight whisper.

"Markie!" she squealed in delight.

His hand tightened on her arm as he prepared to drag her out of the room, but before he could move, she threw her arms around his neck and pressed her barely covered body close.

With some idea of pushing her away, he moved his hands to her waist. A small husky laugh caught in her throat, and a moment later her lips were pressed to his in a kiss as outrageous as her appearance.

Laken had to swallow another laugh when she felt his hard, angry lips under hers. Another man, a less civilized man, would have shoved her away and given her holy hell with the whole restaurant bearing witness. But Marcus was not another man. He was the king of control.

A moment later she caught her breath in surprise as his hands slid to her hips and jerked her tightly against him. His mouth—still hard, still angry—moved on hers in a kiss that suddenly felt real.

Laken fought the need to struggle free of the embrace. She couldn't blow her act. But this wasn't going the way she had planned it. She was supposed to be running the show. It was her plan. Her farce. And there definitely weren't supposed to be any tongues involved.

The kiss finally ended, not because she pulled away but because he decided to end it. Drawing in a slow, bracing breath, she avoided his eyes and took a seat at the table.

"Sorry I'm late," she said, addressing the table at large, her voice annoyingly breathless. "It was a last-minute emergency. My roommate borrowed my favorite blush—twenty-five bucks I spent on that blush—and then she misplaced it."

Laken was recovering her composure, concentrating all her energy on the part she was supposed to be playing. "We finally found it under the couch." Her gaze wandered around the table, lingering on the colorless man to her left. "Well, aren't you a cutie?" She turned her head to wink at his wife. "I'll bet you've had a few catfights over this one. It wouldn't do to tell him though.

Men get so cocky—no pun intended—when they know you're hot for them."

Mr. Jameson's first reaction was to puff up with pride, but then, as he remembered that he was supposed to be insulted, his narrow features stiffened and he shot a furious glance in Marcus's direction.

"Look, guys," Laken said, leaning into the table, "since you've already eaten and I grabbed a chili dog on my way here, what say we blow this joint and go somewhere a little more lively?"

The silence that followed her proposal was a long one. She had time to pull out a pack of chewing gum, offer it around the table, and put a stick in her mouth. Pretending to be oblivious to the three sets of indignant eyes that were trained on her, she blew a small pink bubble then sucked it back in her mouth to pop it.

When the uncomfortable silence continued to draw out, she looked at Mrs. Jameson. "You're looking pale, honey. That time of the month? It gets me that way too. Want us to call you a cab? I can handle these guys." She cast a mischievous glance toward first one man, then the other. "Like I always say, two's company and three's my kind of party."

Laughing at her own joke—she seemed to be only one who appreciated it—she leaned over to place a hand on Mr. Jameson's forearm. "Ever been to the Golden Duck, sugar? It's always crowded, but as it happens, one of the dancers is a dear, dear friend of mine and I'm sure she could get us a table. LaRue and I shared the same man for over a year." She shook her head, exhaling a regretful sigh. "LaRue fell for him. If I've told her once, I've told her a million times. Take the money, do your thing, and have some fun. But don't ever, ever fall for them."

She squirmed in her seat, settling into a more comfortable position. "I have to admit, he was free with his cash. But not nearly as much fun as my Markie here. When money and fun come in one adorable package, I call that lucky."

She sent Marcus a loving look, swallowing a laugh at the evil look in his dark eyes. "You remember LaRue, don't you, baby? I asked you to invite her to your costume party. She came as Marilyn Monroe."

She shifted her gaze to the couple and giggled. "You should have seen this guy. He came as *The Thinker*. It fits, doesn't it? Anyway, he almost caused a riot when he went out and tried to direct traffic." She giggled again. "Stark, staring naked, his cute little tush shining in the streetlight. It cost a few bucks to get him out of that one, I can tell you."

It was during the last few words of her carefully fabricated reminiscence that the Jamesons, with red faces and tight lips, rose in unison to their feet. Two bodies sharing a single brain.

"I think we've finished here," Mr. Jameson

said. "You'll have to go on to the Golden Goose without us."

"Duck," Laken corrected. "The Golden Duck."

Ignoring her, Jameson trained his narrow gaze on Marcus. "You'll hear from me first thing tomorrow morning. And so will the senior partners."

Then he and his wife turned and walked stiffly away.

Laken watched until they had disappeared from sight then glanced at Marcus. He hadn't said a word, but judging by his expression, this was a man with murder on his mind.

Laken rested her elbows on the table and propped her chin on her knuckles. "Hi," she said, sending him a bright smile. "I like that tie."

He stared at her for several tense moments then stood up. Catching her upper arm in a tight grasp, he hauled her to her feet and, still without a word, marched her out of the restaurant.

"Don't you have to pay the bill?" she asked as they passed the maître d'. "I guess not. It must be nice being Marcus Aurelius Reed of the Chicago Reeds. If I tried to walk out on a dinner tab, I'd be flattened by a flying tackle before I got through the door."

Not a word in response. He simply tightened his hold on her arm and nodded to the doorman, who held the door open without evincing a hint of curiosity.

And there wasn't a word from him as they waited for his car to be brought round.

Fifteen minutes later, when he dragged her out of his car and into his house, he still hadn't spoken. He pulled her up a flight of stairs and into a large bedroom, kicking the door closed behind them.

It was obviously the master bedroom. His bedroom. Like the rest of the house it was masculine and filled with antiques. One antique in particular dominated the room. A massive bed with a headboard of intricately carved mahogany that seemed to take up one entire wall.

When he released her arm, Laken muttered, "Oh my," and took an awkward step backward, glancing warily in his direction as he locked the door and pocketed the key.

A moment later she fell into a fit of violent coughing.

Marcus, finally acknowledging her presence, frowned in irritation.

"I swallowed my gum," she explained in a barely audible gasp. "It's your fault for making me nervous."

Reaching out, he thumped her on the back a couple of times. "I suspected you might have a brain somewhere under all that hair. You have a perfect right to be nervous."

"He speaks," she murmured, then studied him from beneath her lashes. "Are you going to murder me?"

"That's something I'll have to think about later. Right now . . ." He reached into his inner breast pocket and pulled out his wallet. "You implied I pay for your services. How much?"

There were two doors in the room. One led to the hall and was locked. The other led either to a bathroom or closet. Whichever it was, it most likely wasn't a way out. Nevertheless Laken began to inch toward it. She was suddenly overcome by the need to put as much distance between herself and that enormous bed as possible.

"Can't you take a joke?" she asked with a weak little smile.

"How much?"

"Look, I don't think—"

He took out several bills. "I have only a couple of hundred in cash. Do you take American Express?"

Placing the money and card on a small table, he took off his jacket and draped it over the back of a chair. After he did the same with his tie, Marcus began to move toward her, slipping his shirt buttons free as he walked.

"Oh, help," Laken said breathlessly, watching as he pulled his shirt free of his slacks and shrugged out of it.

Her back was pressed against the door. Unable to take her eyes off him, she held up one hand. "If you'll just listen to me . . ."

His fingers were on his belt now, deftly unfastening it. "You can talk later. For the present I have other plans."

He slid the belt free of the loops and tossed it toward the chair. "One of us seems to be overdressed," he said, his voice quiet and without inflection. "Your turn, Miss Murphy. Since you're covered by only a few scraps of silk—"

"Polyester," she corrected automatically, her voice thin, her pulse rapid.

"Polyester," he amended as a smile twitched at his strong lips. "As I was saying, since there isn't much of it, you shouldn't have any trouble getting out of it, but I can help if you'd like."

Somehow, at some point, things had gone seriously astray, Laken decided. She had obviously misjudged his tolerance level and pushed him too far. The farce had gotten away from her and it was now his show.

Moistening her lips, she tried to think what to do next. There had to be a way out. She was creative. She could handle this. She would simply—

When both his hands came up to rest on her shoulders, her thoughts scattered to the wind and she panicked. "Oh, jeez. Oh, jeez. Wait . . . wait . . . Marcus, listen . . . no, don't—wait a second . . . let me—"

His mouth cut off the frantic flow of words. The kiss hurt, as did the hands that moved on her body, exploring it with strokes that were intentionally insulting. And even though she knew he was simply paying her back, for a moment Laken was afraid.

And then everything changed. His lips were no longer hard. They were pliant and warm as they moved on hers. Coaxing. Seducing.

The changing signals left her confused in mind and body. She was no longer fighting him. She was responding. Dear God, she was moving against him.

This time when his hands found her breasts, the touch wasn't lewd and insulting. He cupped them gently in his palms and moved his thumbs across the tips that had grown tight and hard.

She exhaled a breathy little moan, and instantly knew that the sound pleased him. His body told her, as did the husky laugh that brushed across the sensitive flesh of her throat.

As disturbing as the things he was doing to her body was her reaction. This wasn't supposed to happen to her. Even men she had dated for months were not allowed to touch her like this. Laken had felt passion, but not once had she been carried away by it. She liked men and enjoyed being close to them, but in every embrace, no matter how pleasurable, she had always been able to pull back when her brain told her she had had enough.

But now her brain—if it still existed—wasn't telling her a blasted thing. Her body had taken over. This man—cold and controlled, enigmatic and unapproachable—had discovered a side of Laken that she hadn't known existed.

How had her hands come to be on his bare chest? The feel of the warm, hard flesh was mesmerizing her, changing reality, making her feel as though this was the first time she had ever been kissed, the first time she had ever been held.

What would have happened next, she would never know because at the moment when her hands began to slide lower, when her thumbs dipped behind the waistband of his slacks, a single, brilliantly clear thought broke through the haze of passion that surrounded her: If she didn't stop this now, there would be no stopping.

With a groan that came from deep in her throat, she pulled free and moved away from him. Closing her eyes, she wiped her mouth with the back of one trembling hand, her breathing labored, her pulse rapid.

When she finally opened her eyes, she forced herself to meet his dark, steady gaze. "You aren't going to rape me," she said in an impossibly husky voice.

Reaching out, he ran one hand down her throat to her breasts, his fingertips brushing lightly across the exposed swell of flesh. "Are you sure of that?"

She moved her head in a short, choppy nod. "Yes." Her voice was stronger now. "Because it's not the civilized thing to do. You wanted to punish me and you did." After letting out a slow, trembling breath, she moved her shoulders in a slight shrug. "I can't blame you for that. I took a shot, you retaliated. That's the way it is in war. But . . . can we talk now?"

When his hand dropped to his side, she released a noisy breath of relief. Although he didn't look all that interested in what she had to say, at least he was moving away from her.

Swinging around, he moved across the room and sat on the bed. As he leaned back against the headboard he watched her straighten her dress and run still-shaking hands through her hair.

Laken swallowed a couple of times then cast a sideways glance in his direction. "I'm sorry I made you lose a client."

He made no reply. He simply stared at her, his expression unchanging, his harsh features carved in granite.

"What I mean is . . ." She exhaled a slow breath. "Okay, I was trying to cause trouble for you and I succeeded, but I didn't think—"

"Again."

Grimacing at the succinct indictment, she moved closer to the bed. "You have a real nice opinion of me, don't you?"

When his only response was a raised brow, she bit her lip and sat on the other side of the bed with her back to him. For a moment she simply stared at the painting on the wall.

"You're right . . . you're right," she said finally. "I've made a mess of it. I didn't think the plan all the way through to the end. It was supposed to be just another way of forcing you to see me so that I could—"

She broke off with a squeal when she found herself jerked backward. And then she was beneath him.

"You're on my bed, Laken," he said in a husky whisper.

He had never called her by her first name before and somehow the sound of it on his lips was more erotic than anything she had experienced tonight.

"Was it an error in strategy?" he continued. "Or have you decided to switch from terrorist tactics to bribery?"

Staring straight into her wide-open eyes, he ran one hand over her tense body. "I can be bribed," he admitted with a laugh as he nipped at her lower lip with strong teeth.

Laken gave her head a little shake, cursing the body that was already responding to his touch.

"Marcus?"

The word was only a little whisper, but something—in her voice or expression—made him pull back and frown down at her.

Raising her eyes to his, she said, "Marcus, can we please talk? Can we forget everything that's happened between us in the past week and talk as equals?"

After staring at her for a moment longer, he

eased away from her and moved to lean against the headboard again.

Her movements made awkward by haste, Laken regained her position on the side of the bed and smoothed the black dress down over her thighs.

Without looking at him, she began to speak. "I know that sometimes I come across as a ditz," she said slowly. "I can't help that. It's my nature. I can think a dozen different things at the same time. I can feel a dozen different emotions at the same time. But that doesn't mean I wasn't serious when I asked for your help."

Pausing, she reached up to scratch the end of her nose with one outrageously red nail. "You're a logical man, and this thing with C.J. isn't logical, so you automatically rejected it. The thing is, I didn't know what you were like when I came to Chicago. I guess I was hoping there was some kind of Hippocratic oath for shamans and that you would help my brother simply because he needed help. Then when I met you and you made it obvious that you had put the past behind you, I had to switch gears fast. I had to wing it."

She shrugged. "I admit it. I screwed up, and because of that, we got off on the wrong foot. But I can't back down simply because I started out wrong."

Moving sideways, she shifted so that she could see his face. "I need your help. You're my only hope." She sent him an apologetic smile. "I can't give up. If we changed places, if it involved someone you loved, someone who depended on you completely, would *you* give up?"

After holding her gaze for a moment, he stood up and walked to the window. With his strong, bare back to her, he pushed the heavy curtain aside and looked out into the darkness.

When the silence drew out, Laken was afraid he wasn't going to answer, but then, without turning around, he said, "No, I don't suppose I would."

Her shoulders slumped as a wave of relief washed over her. This wasn't victory. She knew that. He still hadn't said he would help her, but at least he was finally taking her seriously. He was really listening to her.

After a moment he swung around and leaned against the wall beside the window. "That was a nice, rational speech you gave just now, but if you cut it down to the bare bones, basically what you're saying is you're going to keep harassing me until I agree to help you. Isn't that right?"

She glanced down at her clasped hands then raised her head again and sent him a helpless look. "I really am sorry that I'm disrupting your life but—"

"But you've got a mission." His lips twisted in a wry smile. "Yes, I think I'm finally beginning to understand that."

When he added nothing else, Laken held her breath. His gaze moved restlessly over her face, a frown furrowing his brow. She wished she knew what he thought of the whole thing. It was a good sign that he was thinking about it at all, she told herself silently, but she still wished she knew exactly what.

"Okay, you win."

A moment passed before she understood what he had said. She rose to her feet and walked around the end of the bed, moving toward him, drawn toward him. "You mean—"

He nodded. "I'll go with you. I'll put on a show that will convince your brother that I'm an authentic shaman, capable of breaking ancient spells. Don the old loincloth, shake some bones, the whole nine yards."

Excitement rushed through her veins. It was really going to happen. C.J. would believe and allow himself to heal. He would be a little boy again. A little boy with a future.

She ran a shaking hand across her face and then sent him a brilliant smile. "I don't know what to say. How can I ever thank you?"

"I haven't done anything yet. Save your gratitude until we see if this works."

Laken barely heard him. Already, she was making plans. "How long will it take you to clear your calendar?" Rubbing her chin in concentration, she glanced at him. "I'll book our flight back to Dallas first thing in the morning. I left my car at the house, so we'll have to take a cab to

Allen." A breathless little laugh escaped her. "I can't wait to call home to tell Rose and C.J. all—"

"Laken."

When she sent him a questioning look, he said, "I'm afraid you don't understand. It's not going to happen in Allen. I have to go back to those hills in West Texas."

After taking a moment to assimilate the information, she nodded. "That makes sense. Okay, I'll call Rosemary and tell her to take C.J. to that little motel on the park grounds. We can meet them there. Rose can stay at the motel while the three of us—"

She broke off when she saw him shaking his head. "No? Why?"

"There's no need for your brother to be at the site just yet. This is not going to be simple and it's not going to be quick," he told her. "There's a cleansing process that has to take place first. It takes several days to become one with the earth."

"I can see how it would." Her voice was distracted as she once again rearranged her plans. "Okay, so Rosemary, C.J., and I will wait at the motel until you're through, then we can join you when—"

He was shaking his head again. Even though she tightened her lips against it, a sound of exasperation escaped her. "What else?"

He raised one brow. "Do you want me to do this?"

"Sorry." She reached up to push the curls off her forehead. "I didn't mean to sound irritable. Of course it has to be done your way. Tell me what you want me to do."

"That's better," he said. "C.J. will stay in Allen with your friend until we need him. As for you, you'll be with me, up in the hills."

"I will?" Her voice sounded as uncertain as she felt. "What do I have to do with it?"

"The patient is supposed to go through a cleansing process as well. Fortunately for us, there happens to be a loophole. If the patient isn't well enough to do it, then the responsibility falls on his closest living relative. I assume that's you."

She nodded, biting her lip.

He studied her face for a moment. "Do you have some objection to that?" he asked quietly.

"No . . . no, I've been meaning to become one with the earth for years. But what with one thing and another, there just never seemed to be time." She glanced at him. "This cleansing thing, is it going to be painful? I mean, you won't have to draw blood or anything?"

His lips spread in a slow smile. "I promise it won't be any worse than what you've put me through in the past week and a half."

She swallowed in an audible gulp. She wasn't at all sure she trusted the look in his dark eyes, but all she managed to say was, "I see."

Moving a step closer, he ran one finger slowly across her cheek. "There's an old saying. You may have heard it. It warns you to be careful what you ask of the gods. You just might get it."

Now Laken was positive. She definitely didn't trust the look in his eyes. But there was nothing she could do about it. Marcus was calling the shots now.

They were going together to the hills of West Texas.

SEVEN

Laken glanced at her watch then shifted her weight from one foot to the other.

She stood on the sidewalk in front of a rustic little store, a combination trading post and coffee shop. Behind the store was a small motel. To the west, in the far distance, mountains of bare, weathered rock rose toward a clear blue sky. To the east it was flat as far as the eye could see. Everything, both the near and the far, had the same rugged look, and all of it composed a whole that was bigger than some Eastern European countries.

Laken had dressed for comfort, just as Marcus had instructed. With frayed denim shorts she wore a green cotton T-shirt that was two sizes too large and running shoes that had not been expensive but fit the shape of her feet without being pumped. She wore sunglasses and a cap with A-1 AUTO PARTS on the front. Her auburn hair was pulled up in a ponytail. On the sidewalk beside her was a canvas carryall.

Now all she needed was a ride.

Shifting her weight back to her right foot, she checked her watch and found that three whole minutes had passed since she last checked it. It was now a quarter to eight. He had said he would be here by eight.

After scratching her nose and checking her pockets to see if she had any wafers left, she shifted her position again. This time, however, she didn't follow the action by immediately glancing at her watch. Instead she whistled a few bars of "What's It All About, Alfie?" before checking the time.

Variety, after all, was the spice of life.

After leaving Chicago three days earlier, Laken had gone home to Allen. She checked in with her boss and took care of things that needed taking care of. Mostly, she spent time with C.J., making him laugh by recapping her adventures in Chicago, telling him about the proposed trip that would take her back to West Texas, to the foothills of the mountains of Big Bend.

Although they would use the archaeological site for the ritual of healing, Marcus had explained that a more isolated spot was required for the preliminaries, somewhere away from park personnel and curious tourists.

Isolated was not a comfortable word, Laken

decided now. It was the kind of word a civilized woman did her best to avoid.

On their earlier trip here, Laken and C.J. had stayed in a rented RV at one of the park's designated camping areas. Lots of company and all the conveniences of home. This time would be different.

The minute he had agreed to help her, Marcus had taken over. The campsite, transportation and camping gear, permission to visit the archaeological dig after the cleansing process was complete, he would take care of everything.

Although Marcus would know best what kind of supplies they needed for the trip, it bothered Laken that he was using his money, and before leaving Chicago, she had made sure he understood that she wanted receipts for everything.

Just as she had decided it was time to shift her position and check her watch again, she heard the sound of a car. Seconds later a brand-new, glossy red Jeep pulled up to the sidewalk near where she stood.

With an apprehensive "oh my," Laken picked up her bag and stepped up to the passenger side of the open vehicle.

Sliding her sunglasses down to the end of her nose, she looked at him. "Please, please tell me you didn't buy this. When I said you should keep all the receipts—"

"Calm down," Marcus said, his dark gaze examining her, assessing her appearance. "I borrowed it from a friend."

Laken exhaled a small, relieved whoosh of air and threw the carryall into the back.

As she climbed in and closed the door behind her, she glanced at the three small cardboard boxes in the back of the Jeep then turned her gaze to the man in the driver's seat.

"It's amazing how those cute little pop-up tents can fit into such teeny boxes," she said hopefully.

"My ancestors didn't use cute little pop-up tents. In fair weather, they slept under the stars, absorbing the night through their skin, feeling the earth under and around them."

"And crawling over them," she muttered under her breath.

Oh yes, she told herself, this trip was definitely going to be different from the last one.

Moments later, when the Jeep turned off the paved highway onto a road that was nothing more than a clear space between the underbrush, she surreptitiously studied the man beside her. This was the first time she had seen him wear anything other than a suit, but whoever said clothes make the man obviously had never met Marcus Aurelius Reed. He was just as distant, just as unapproachable in jeans and chambray shirt as he had been in his Brooks Brothers suits.

"Will I do?" he asked without taking his gaze from the dusty road.

"You still don't look like a medicine man."

"I'm saving the war paint and braids for later."

The dry note in his voice made Laken frown. "Was that a clumsy thing for me to say?" She sighed. "I guess it was. When you haven't been exposed to a culture, when you haven't done some deep thinking and walked a mile in their shoes, it's too easy to say the wrong thing."

Still frowning in concentration, she shifted in the seat, curling one foot beneath her. "It seems to me," she said, "that labels, no matter how politically correct they are, draw lines between groups of people. I know there are good, solid reasons for the labels—ethnic pride, cultural awareness, and like that—but I don't see why we can't have those things and still feel allegiance for the larger group. Mankind. Rather than concentrating on the things that separate us, we should start looking at the things that tie us together. The biggest stumbling block to that happening is that there are too many groups that have been sabotaged by other groups, the ones who happened to be in power. Before we can all just be people, without big old walls between us, everyone has to be standing in the same spot. Even-steven. Which is a thing a lot of people don't want to happen, so each of the short-shafted groups has to work to get the group as whole . . ."

The words suddenly faded away. As usual

when Laken started rambling, she lost all sense of time and place, so she was surprised to find that the Jeep had stopped and Marcus had turned in the seat, one arm wrapped around the steering wheel as he stared at her.

Wriggling in discomfort, she muttered, "Just a theory."

"Right," he said, and opened the door to step out.

She got out as well and glanced around at the site he had chosen. Not that there was all that much to see. They were on a rise that seemed to be the upper edge of a boulder, if a rock the size of a shopping mall could be called a boulder. The only vegetation was dusty-looking grass and stubby little flowering plants that sprang from cracks in the rock.

To the west, the stone surface rose gradually and continued to rise as far as she could see. To the east, in the near distance, she could see the tops of trees.

"We're not far from the trading post, are we?" she said, trying not to sound too relieved.

"Five or six miles," he told her as he began to move toward the trees.

Shoving her hands in her back pockets, she followed. Less than fifty yards from the Jeep, the rock face abruptly dropped away. Below, in a narrow valley, the clear water of a shallow stream slipped over pale rocks, cutting a winding path through stands of cottonwood and willows.

She glanced at him. "Are we going to camp down there, on the creek bank?"

"No."

Laken waited, certain other words would accompany the gruff monosyllable. She was wrong.

"Okeydokey," she said under her breath.

So he wasn't in a chatty mood. That was fine with her. She was here for one reason and one reason only, to make sure C.J. got well. From now on, she would simply keep her mouth shut.

It was a fine resolution, but given her nature, impossible to keep. A moment later, when her imagination was captured by the mystery and majesty of the broken landscape, she didn't even remember making it.

"Did they really live in these hills? Those mystics, I mean."

He moved his shoulders in a slight shrug as he turned and headed back for the Jeep. "For your brother's sake, we're going to pretend they did."

"You know, don't you?" she asked, trailing along behind him. "You know who and what they were. You know exactly where they lived out their lives." When he didn't answer, she added, "But you're going to keep the truth to yourself, just like Joseph Two Trees did."

Ignoring her, he moved to the back of the open vehicle. "We might as well get started."

"You mean the cleansing? Absolutely." Laken nodded in agreement then repeated, "Absolutely." She paused. "How do we do that?"

His only response was to lean over, take two hatchets from one of the boxes, and hand one to Laken.

"Ye old tomahawk," she said, staring down at it. "Are we making war on someone? A Boy Scout troop that seriously annoyed you? Or has that wascally wabbit been hanging around again?"

"We're gathering willow branches. An inch to an inch and a half in diameter." Even as he spoke he was moving back toward the slope that would take them down to the stream. "Ten or twelve feet long."

Skipping to keep up, she said, "These are dead branches you're talking about, right? We find them on the ground and use our trusty little axes to whack them down to size."

"The wood has to be pliable. Which means we get them directly from the tree."

Frowning, she used the blunt edge of the hatchet to scratch the back of her leg. "Isn't there some kind of law against that? Won't we be desecrating government property or something?"

"Trees don't belong to the government."

Laken did a little hop-skip to catch up again. "I'm not sure that's the official opinion."

"It's my opinion, and what's more important, it's the trees' opinion. Trees belong to themselves and they won't mind my taking what I need."

She raised one brow, a gesture of skepticism that he missed because he was ahead of her again.

"They told you this? You discussed this issue with the trees and they said, 'Go ahead, Marcus old man, hack off some of our extremities. We'll clear it with Parks and Wildlife."

Exhaling a rough sound of exasperation, he stopped so abruptly, she almost ran into him. Turning to face her, he said, "As a Native American I have certain rights." When she opened her mouth to make another objection, he added, "I got permission, okay."

Without waiting for her response, he began to make his way down the rock-strewn slope.

Because he had sounded just a tad irritated, Laken decided the prudent thing would be to gather her branches from the trees on the opposite side of the stream. Listed somewhere in her rules for survival was, "Never annoy a man with an ax in his hand."

Due to the fact that she had never used a hatchet before, she approached the task with hesitancy, but it didn't take long for her to figure out that hesitancy wasn't going to get the job done. So after sending up a prayer for the safety of her fingers, she grasped a limb with her left hand and began to swing the little ax with vigor.

After half an hour she had four limbs of just exactly the right diameter and length, and when Marcus called her name, she was feeling more than a little pleased with herself.

"Let's carry what we have to the top," he said

when she joined him. "Then I can—" He broke off. "What's wrong now?"

She was staring at the pile of willow branches beside him. There must have been at least thirty or forty of them.

Something was very wrong here. He wasn't even breathing hard and he had enough for a bonfire. She had blisters on the palms of her hands and perspiration running into her eyes. And she had four limbs.

"Nothing," she said finally. "You go ahead. I'll grab some of mine and follow you."

Moments later, as she added an armload of his branches to hers she told herself that it wasn't stealing, and if she didn't identify them as hers, it couldn't even be considered lying. Not really.

It took her another five minutes to half drag, half carry the unwieldy bundle to the top of the slope. Glancing around, she spotted him twenty feet or so beyond the Jeep at a spot where the rock thrust abruptly upward.

After placing the branches on top of the ones he had carried, she rubbed at the scratches on her arms. "Now what?"

"You go get more branches while I build."

Stifling a groan at the thought of hauling up more wood, she said, "What are you building?"

"A sweat lodge, to rid myself of the impurities of the world. Get more branches."

After making a vulgar gesture, which once again he didn't see, she made her way back down the ravine. Each time she brought more wood, the thing he was bending and twisting and wrapping had grown more solid.

As the morning wore on and the hut began to take shape, Marcus would occasionally stop working and focus his gaze on some distant point, his head tilted slightly, as though he were listening, searching for a sound or shift in the wind. After a moment he would give his head a small shake and go back to work. Whatever he heard—or didn't hear—didn't improve his disposition.

It was getting close to noon when Laken dropped to the warm rock surface beside the hut and wiped perspiration from her face.

"Want to switch?" she asked, pulling her damp shirt away from her midriff. "I'll knit the sweatshop—"

"Sweat lodge."

"—and you can take my place toting that barge and lifting that bale."

He didn't answer immediately. He kept working, but after a while, without looking at her, he said, "In the days when the Old Ones were alive, the women were the workers. They fetched and carried. They cooked and cleaned. They bore children and raised them. They scraped buffalo hides and chewed them until they were soft. But mostly they stayed out of the way and kept their mouths shut." He glanced over his shoulder at her. "Why do you think they call them the good old days?"

Although she knew the words were designed to annoy her, she was too hot and tired to do more than throw a small twig at him as she rose to her feet and once again headed for the stream.

By the time they broke for lunch—canned wieners and crackers—the skeleton of the sweat lodge was complete. It was approximately five feet in diameter and around the inner edge he had arranged a layer of willow leaves. In the center, on the rock floor, he had built a small fire. Beside the fire was a container of water.

After lunch, when the dry wood had mostly burned away, he placed several flat rocks atop the glowing coals then spread a blue plastic tarp over the wooden frame.

He had ignored her when she complimented him on how quickly he had put the thing together. And he had ignored her when, in a fit of pique, she told him his precious hut looked like an igloo for Smurfs. He was getting real good at ignoring her.

Marcus was here against his will. She knew that. They weren't friends. They barely qualified as acquaintances. She acknowledged that fact as well. And he had every reason in the world to hold a grudge against her.

Rising to her feet, she made one more trip down to the ravine, to a spring she had discovered earlier. Dipping into the ice-cold water, she washed her face and hands, letting the moisture slide down her neck. Then she drank deeply.

Rocking back on her heels, she scolded herself for having felt sorry for herself. In Chicago, she had vowed to do anything to help her brother. A couple of days in the wilderness with old Stone Face wasn't so much.

Her spirits lifting, she began to the climb to the top, singing "Do You Love Me Now that I Can Dance?" complete with choreography as she went.

The words faded when she reached camp and Marcus was nowhere in sight. Instantly, the hair rose on the back of her neck.

Glancing around, she whispered, "Marcus?"

"What?"

Startled, she swung around. He was a couple of feet behind her, moving toward the sweat lodge. And except for the white towel draped around his hips, he was naked.

There wasn't an ounce of spare flesh on him. His chest was dark and hard and free of hair. Although the muscles that gleamed in the afternoon sun were well defined, they weren't knotted like those of weight lifters, which looked like something foreign that had been added on. They were smooth and hard, part of him.

"You wanted something?"

Pulling her gaze away from the towel hanging low on his hips, Laken gave her head one short shake. "No. Uh-uh. Nothing. I was just . . . you know . . . wondering where you were."

He held her gaze for just a moment longer,

then moved past her and pulled the tarp aside, stooping to enter the sweat lodge.

Laken simply stood where she was. It was quite a while before she let out the breath she had been holding and wiped her damp palms on the sides of her shorts.

"Okay," she said hoarsely then, raising her voice, "I guess you're going to sweat awhile. That's good." She scratched the tip of her nose then her chin. "I think I'll go exploring while you're in there . . . um . . . sweating. Okay, Marcus?" She paused. "Okay," she said, as though he had actually answered her.

Inside the hut, Marcus sat cross-legged on a layer of leaves. Reaching out, he poured a stream of water onto the hot rocks. Steam hissed upward, filling his nostrils, moistening his face.

He closed his eyes and rested his hands palms up on his knees. A moment later, when he heard Laken walk away, still muttering to herself, he leaned his head back and gave a soft chuckle.

Laken stood beside the campfire, poking at it with a stick as she watched Marcus, fully clothed now, stoop beside a box of supplies.

"I'd be glad to help," she told him. "I know you were teasing about women doing all the work, chewing buffalo hide and all, but I'm perfectly willing to help." She paused. "The thing is, I can't cook."

He glanced up at her. "I take it C.J. is a thin child."

She laughed. "No, the good thing about growing boys is they'll eat anything."

"I'll cook."

"Wise decision," she said, nodding. "You cook. I'll clean up."

Dinner was some sort of stew, more crackers, and steaming hot cups of coffee. By the time Laken had cleaned the utensils at the stream and used the opportunity to wash up and change into a sweatsuit, darkness had fallen. When she returned to the campfire, she took a place on the opposite side from Marcus, who was silently drinking another cup of coffee.

"I can't have more than one cup of coffee at night," she said in an attempt at pleasant conversation. "The caffeine makes me hyper."

As she had expected, there was no response. Stubbornly, she tried again. "This is nice. Peaceful. Are we going to sing 'Kum Ba Ya' now?"

Although he glanced at her, one brow raised, he made no comment.

Exhaling a small sigh, she picked up her poking stick and gave the fire some more attention. She wriggled a bit to find a comfortable position then poked some more, humming "Kum Ba Ya" under her breath just to annoy him.

Gradually the flickering flames, the night breeze, and the sky full of stars began to work their magic. Now it truly was peaceful. And when she allowed the peace to reach her, Laken realized she was dead tired.

"I think you'd better go to bed before you fall face-first in the fire."

Her eyes jerked open and she blinked sleepily at the man across the fire. Smiling, she said, "I don't want to dampen the party spirit we've got going here, but you may be right."

He rose to his feet in one fluid movement and walked to the back of the Jeep.

"Marcus," she called after him, "what's your Comanche name?"

"Three Dog Night," he said, his voice dry as he tossed her a rolled sleeping bag. "Can you open it, or do you want me to help?"

"I'm not completely helpless. I think I can manage to untie a couple of strings." She shot a look in his direction. "Your ancestors used down-filled sleeping bags?"

"No. And they didn't eat freeze-dried stew either, but the details don't matter. Whatever they ate and whatever they slept on, they did it out here, under these same stars. The essence is the same."

It was almost a conversation, she decided as she shook out the sleeping bag. Enough of a conversation for her to feel a little triumphant as she wriggled into the bag.

A second later she got up, removed several rocks from under the bag, then slid in again.

Several feet away she heard the rustle of nylon

as Marcus moved restlessly inside the matching bag. When she had listened to the rustling stop and start again several times, she rolled over and said, "Why don't you just get up and move the rocks like I did?"

"There are no rocks. It's the silence. It's too loud. Too crowded," he said, his voice irritable. Then, as though he had given too much away, he turned over, presenting her with a view of his back. "Go to sleep."

Too crowded. Was that what he had been listening to all day, echoes of the past? She hadn't thought of that. Could it be possible that this was the first time he had been in the wilds since he had lived with his grandfather? Was he remembering those days, thinking about how he had cut himself off from his roots?

Whatever the problem was, it didn't sound like fun. There was something in his voice she had never heard before. It was barely detectable, but in a man like Marcus, the difference was enormous. He had almost sounded vulnerable.

Somehow, right at this moment, he reminded her of C.J. Her brother had a complex mind. Because he comprehended more, there was more for him to worry about. Too much for a twelve-year-old. Whenever Laken saw the tension building in her brother, she played the court jester. She sat by his bed and amused him with brainless anecdotes until he was relaxed enough to sleep.

"Did I ever tell you about my cat?"

A soft, abrupt laugh from the other sleeping bag made her raise her head. "What's funny?" she asked.

"I was just thinking about all the things that have happened since I met you, beginning with the way you lied to get in to see me and ending with the way you chased off a damn good client."

"What does that have to do with my cat?"

"Given the circumstances, 'Did I ever tell you about my cat?' seemed a little peculiar, like a surreal painting where antithetical objects occupy the same space."

"Exactly the effect I was going for," she said, her voice dry. "Does this mean you don't want to hear about Cerberus?"

After a slight pause, he said, "Why does it not surprise me that you have a cat named after the three-headed dog that guards the entrance to hell?"

"C.J. renamed him several years ago. I think it has something to do with the way the stupid cat hangs around in the bushes by the porch and sort of springs out of the darkness just in time to scare the bejeebers out of our visitors. But it's not just the way he appears from out of nowhere, it's the way he looks. He's bald. Well, not totally bald. If he were totally bald, I could tell people he was one of those grotesquely expensive show cats, but he's managed to keep a few mangy patches of fur. Just enough to make him look truly evil."

"I can see how that would put a damper on your social life."

Although she still heard reluctance in his voice, he was definitely loosening.

"Social life?" she repeated, smiling at the small victory. "I don't think people in my income bracket have social lives. We just have friends. And all of our friends hate Cerberus. Luckily that doesn't stop them from coming to the house. They just make the sign of the cross and sneak past him."

"What about dates? Or don't people in your income bracket date new men? Maybe you can afford only secondhand models."

She laughed. "That's one for you. When, on the rare occasion I date someone new, he has to pass the Cerberus test first. Only those with a true heart and low blood pressure make it past him." She smiled. "He was Mama's cat. He lost his hair after my parents died. I assumed it was grief." She paused for a moment, remembering, then shook her head. "Of course, I could never get the vet to confirm that theory. He said it was either an allergy or nerves."

"He lives with you. I vote for nerves."

"Funny."

After a slight pause, he said, "You still miss your parents. I can hear it in your voice."

"Sure I miss them. Don't you miss your grandfather?"

The silence that followed her question let her

know she had messed up. He had been relaxing, but now the tension was back. She could feel it in the air between them.

"My parents were both wonderful people," she said quickly, making an attempt to recover lost ground. "Daddy was a big man. Not just tall. Big. And he had an Irish temper. Did I tell you he was a cop? It was all he ever wanted to be and he was good at it. He could stop a riot by himself, using nothing but his bare fists. But I never saw him raise a hand to anyone smaller or more helpless.

"Mama was completely opposite. She was always a little vague. Fey is what Daddy called her. He said she was a lovely woman who lived in a lovely world, a place those of us with two feet on the ground could never visit. But she was a good mother. Daddy was practical. He wanted everything spelled out so he could deal with it. Mama went more on feelings. You didn't have to tell her if something was wrong. She always knew, and she was always there to help."

Although he didn't respond, she sensed that the tension was losing its grip on him. It was strange how she could read his mood so well after having known him only a short time.

"My parents were perfect together," she continued. "They had been married only a year when I came along. They wanted to get started early so they could have a houseful of kids, but it didn't happen. Mama didn't get pregnant again until I was almost thirteen, so when C.J. came along, I was like a third parent, all of us spoiling him, all of us loving him."

She smiled, thinking back to those long ago days. "Around that time—and it may have been a sign of how deeply this beautiful baby affected me—I decided I would become a lawyer and specialize in children's rights."

"What changed your mind?"

Her eyes closed briefly in relief. It was crazy how his question felt like a victory, as though taking his mind off his problems was important. Really important.

"I didn't change my mind," she told him, keeping her voice even. "It's still what I want. I was in my first semester of college when my parents were killed."

"Couldn't you have stayed in, used the insurance money for tuition? I assume your parents had life insurance."

"There was insurance and the policeman's fund, but it still wasn't enough to pay for child care, college, and household expenses. If I had stayed in school and got a job to cover the rest, it would have left me no time to be with C.J. He was five years old and had just lost his mother and father. He needed me. I was lucky enough to find the job I have now. Bud, the owner, let me keep C.J. at work with me. It's a good job. Good people. I can wait until C.J. is grown to go back to school. Even if it means I'll be the oldest living American to ever take the bar exam."

"Amazing. You don't even resent having to put your life on hold for your brother," he said with quiet astonishment.

"Resent C.J.?" she asked with equal amazement. "Why should I? He didn't ask me to do anything. I simply did what was necessary. I've always believed that every adult has a responsibility to every child, so how much more do I owe my own brother?"

He was quiet for a while, as though assimilating the information, then he said, "You said you date only occasionally. You're a beautiful woman. I assume restricting your personal life is also something you do for your brother."

Although the beautiful-woman part gave Laken a little thrill, the rest of it brought a frown. "You make it sound like I decided to sit on the porch with that demented cat until C.J. is grown. It's not like that. We get together with people who have kids and do family things. Sometimes, when C.J. is sleeping over at a friend's house, I go out with my unmarried friends or accept a date with someone new.

"The truth is, if you met the last three men I dated, you'd see that opting out of the single life is no hardship. Bob and Harry and Ted. What a trio. Bob gave up job after job because they were intruding on his attempts to read the future by studying the alignment of hair on his forearms. A sweet man with only three brain cells between him and a can of Spam. Then there was Harry-Poor-Harry who didn't know why his last two wives left him. His first didn't leave. He left her. Because his mother told him to, which gives you a pretty good idea of why the last two left." She paused. "And that brings us to Ted. Ted had a problem with other people's feelings. He admitted other people probably had feelings, he just didn't know what that had to do with him."

"Losers," was the succinct indictment that came out of the darkness.

Laken's lips curved in a small smile. "I guess that gives us something in common. Your women are losers as well. They all managed to lose you fast enough."

"How do you know that?"

"I have my sources." Shifting her position, she propped her head on her forearm. "That night I showed up at the restaurant, I knew in advance that it was business. If you had been out with a woman, I would never have done it."

"Because?" he said with some irritation. "I assume there's a point to that revelation?"

"There is. The point is, if you had been with a woman, it wouldn't have worked. You wouldn't have cared what she thought of you. It wouldn't have bothered you a bit if she got up and walked out and you never saw her again."

The nylon rustled as he shifted his position.

"Pretty harsh judgment for a woman who keeps picking dipsticks."

"Maybe. But you see, if they hadn't been dipsticks, I wouldn't have chosen them. My problem is, I have a savior complex. And two of those men I actually helped."

"Let me guess. Ted was the holdout."

"It didn't take much brain power to figure that one out," she said with a soft laugh. "Ted was too far gone by the time I met him. I could have sat around waiting for him to get real until I grew a dowager's hump, which, by the way, I used to think was pity sex for old ladies."

When she heard his chuckle, she smiled in pleasure. "It put me off men for a while."

"Understandable."

Laken raised her head, peering through the darkness. She had lost him again. Something in his voice, a certain stiffness, made it clear his thoughts were straying back to the unknown problem he had been wrestling with all day.

When this happened with C.J., Laken always beefed up the story. She would add a few small fabrications to recapture his interest. The extra bits usually had to do with the cranky old man who lived down the street from them. She would swear to her brother that she had seen a monstrous face at Mr. Leggit's basement window or that she had heard unearthly screams coming from his house when she passed by at night. Although C.J. knew very well she was making it all up, the stories always captured his attention, amusing him against his will.

Laken was pretty sure monsters wouldn't work with Marcus, but she was nothing if not imaginative. She would simply improvise.

"I almost considered switching to women," she said, her voice matter-of-fact.

A choking sound came from his direction, and he abruptly rolled over to face her. "Are you—do you find yourself physically attracted to other women?"

Laken almost laughed aloud. He was well and truly hooked.

"No," she said. "And that was the second reason I decided it probably wasn't right for me."

"Second? What was number one?"

"The Bitch Factor."

"I beg your pardon?"

"Women compete with other women. We can't help it, it's the way we're made. I don't see how another woman could look at me without my clothes and not think, 'Mine are bigger than hers, ha-ha.' Or 'If she's a size five, I'm Snow White.' "

His laugh was more animated now, more liberated, and the sound warmed her from the inside out.

"And there's no mystery," she went on, her voice growing softer. "Women know what women think. And we know how a woman's body works. But to men, we're this wonderful, enigmatic 'other.' The mystery keeps them off balance. They can't get complacent because they never know what they're dealing with. Of course, it works the other way too. Women don't understand the male mind. And although the male body can sometimes be intimidating, it can also be a beautiful thing."

Even as she said the words a vision rose in her mind and she saw once again the way he had looked earlier today when nothing covered his body but a towel and her gaze.

"A beautiful thing," she repeated in a husky whisper.

In the next few minutes a gentle quietness fell between them, and then he said, "Good night, Laken."

As she snuggled down in the sleeping bag Laken told herself that she had only imagined she heard gratitude in the words.

Marcus lay on his back, one arm folded beneath his head as he stared up at the stars. He could tell by Laken's breathing that she had fallen asleep.

She was an amazing woman, he told himself with a small smile. Telling him bedtime stories to help him relax. It must be the savior complex she had talked about.

The thought brought a frown of displeasure. Marcus didn't need saving. And he didn't want to be grateful to her. He didn't want to be attracted to her.

He didn't want to be here.

When Old Joe's face flashed across his mind, Marcus ruthlessly cut off the memory.

This was the reason he had fought against helping her. The memories.

Two nights in a row Marcus had had a dream that hadn't come to him in years. In the dream he was twelve, and he was running so hard, he thought his heart would burst. He was trying to catch up with—

He didn't want to think about the dream, or any of the other memories that all day had been trying to get at him, taunting him, crowding his mind. Memories that came with the landscape.

So why was he here?

It wasn't what Laken thought. She hadn't forced him into it. He could have gotten rid of her with very little trouble. But it was simpler to pretend, even to himself, that she had blackmailed him into coming than to face the truth. That something inside him, something he didn't understand and didn't want to examine, had forced him to come here.

Maybe it was the woman who was sleeping a few feet away. Maybe it was the past pulling at him. Maybe it was a combination of the two.

It was something Marcus would have to sort out while he was here.

EIGHT

Laken sat on a rock, her elbows on her knees, a plastic mug of coffee cradled between her hands. It was early enough that a slight chill still hung in the air, but she knew from experience that before long the day would turn hot.

Marcus was in the sweat lodge. Again. In the past two days he had spent half his waking time there. The other half he had spent ignoring Laken.

When she heard the rustle of the plastic tarp, she turned her head in that direction. By now she should be used to seeing his half-naked body, but the sight of his bare flesh, tanned and hard, glistening with damp heat, always brought a strange little flush of pleasure.

"I'll be gone most of the day," he said a few minutes later as he joined her. The towel was gone and he now wore jeans and T-shirt. "I've decided it was time I went off to communicate with the earth."

"Give it my best," she said, then as he turned to leave: "What's your Comanche name?"

"Spread Eagle," he said without looking back.

Giving a soft chuckle, she shifted her position so that she could watch him climb the rocky rise behind camp. Moments later he was out of sight.

Marcus breathed evenly as he climbed. To his surprise, he had found that pacing himself came as naturally as breathing. Apparently when you were trained by Joseph Two Trees, you stayed trained.

He had been climbing steadily for almost two hours when he finally found a place that would serve his purpose. The rock face jutted out sharply, forming a narrow balcony that overlooked the barren world below.

As he stared out across the terrain spreading out like a brown-and-tan blanket, a peculiar feeling of disorientation washed over him.

Why in hell was he here? What was he hoping to accomplish?

He had come awake well before dawn, feeling restless and agitated, as though something he couldn't see were pulling at him. The hills, said a voice in the back of his mind. The hills were calling to him.

Now, in full daylight, the idea seemed more

than a little ridiculous. These hills, a prologue to the mountain range farther west, were nothing more than piles of rocks looking down on sand and dusty tumbleweeds.

After running restless fingers through his perspiration-dampened hair, he closed his eyes and made a conscious effort to separate himself from all thought. His chest rose and fell as he drew in deep drafts of air. Again and again, he fought to free his mind of the restrictions imposed by the world he had been living in for the past twenty-five years.

Finally he opened his eyes and, keeping his gaze on the horizon, reached down to strip off his shoes and socks. Then he pulled the T-shirt over his head, dropped it to the rock surface, and began to move forward.

At the very edge, he stopped and raised his face to the sun. It was approaching midday, and the heat was a solid thing that pricked at his bare flesh. He heard the distant cry of birds and caught the scent of creosote in the air. The earth was speaking to him.

For a long time he simply stood there, listening.

It was late afternoon before Laken saw Marcus striding back toward camp.

She knew immediately that something had changed. It was in the way he moved, in the way he held himself, as though whatever he had experienced during the day had allowed him to fit more comfortably inside his own skin.

When he reached her, he met her eyes and said, "Now it begins."

Laken cocked her head to the side, listening for the dramatic swell of music that should have accompanied the words. After a moment she rose slowly to her feet, pushed her hands into the back pockets of her shorts, and met his gaze.

Something was different there as well. If she hadn't known better, she would have said amusement was gleaming in his brown-black eyes. Whatever it was, it made her uneasy.

"Now it begins," she repeated slowly. "You mean my part?" When he nodded, she nodded as well. "Great. I'm ready for action. Lead me to it."

He raised one dark brow. "You don't sound ready. You sound more like Joan of Arc facing the flames."

Laken's eyes narrowed as she studied his features. "Why did you bring her up? Does my part have something to do with fire?" Shifting her weight from one foot to the other, she tried for an ingratiating smile. "Not many people know this, I mean, it's something that I keep pretty well hidden, but—the thing is, I'm a real baby about pain."

The dark brow rose higher. "Are you trying to back out?"

"No . . . no, of course not. This is what I came for." She paused and cleared her throat. "What do I have to do?"

"Stop worrying. It doesn't have anything to do with fire." He rubbed his chin, his expression reflective as he watched her. "Did you ever see the movie *A Man Called Horse?*"

"*A Man Called—*" Laken broke off with a squeal of alarm. "The one where they stuck barbs in his chest and strung him from the ceiling?" She crossed her arms over her breasts in a defensive move. "I don't even have pierced ears. Don't you think that's a little—"

She broke off again, tilting her head to the side as she watched him. He was laughing. Marcus Aurelius Reed was laughing. And this wasn't a little chuckle. He was leaning against the Jeep, his body shaking with helpless laughter.

An answering smile twitched at her lips as she slapped his arm. "That was cold. That was really cold."

He straightened away from the Jeep, wiping his eyes with the tips of his fingers. "Sorry, I couldn't resist."

"Next time try harder," she said, her voice dry. "So what do I have to do?"

Moving to the back of the Jeep, he dug around in a canvas duffel bag. A moment later he pulled something out and handed it to her.

Laken stared at it. "A bathing suit? The next

part of the ritual is going for a swim? Isn't the stream a little shallow for that?"

"We're not going down to the stream." He nodded in the opposite direction. "We're going up."

They climbed for over half an hour, and although the going was rough, he made no attempt to help her. As she made her way over and around car-sized boulders, she frequently lost sight of her guide. Then she would round a bend and find him waiting patiently for her to catch up.

She had fallen behind again when she heard him call, "This is it."

When she reached him, Laken found that he was standing on a rock terrace approximately twenty feet wide and fifty feet long. Although the shelf was level, the rock floor beneath her feet wasn't flat. Centuries of wind and rain had weathered it, leaving a smooth but pitted surface. Some of the depressions were no more than a couple of inches deep, others sank down in foot-deep potholes.

As she followed Marcus's gaze she caught a flash of silver. It was water, glinting in the sun.

Moving closer, she saw that the sides of three of the basins had been worn away until they were interconnected, making a cloverleaf pool, eight feet across at its widest.

"Nature's bathtub," she said in delight. "Where did the water come from? Is there a spring?"

He shook his head. "No, it rained up here last night. When I saw it on my way up, I knew it would be the perfect place for you to bathe me."

Choking on an indrawn breath, Laken cleared her throat vigorously. Maybe she hadn't heard him right.

"A perfect place for—" she began slowly. "We climbed halfway to Jupiter so I can give you a bath?"

His strong lips twitched in a smile that held far too much amusement. "You got it."

"This is part of the ritual?" She didn't bother to hide her skepticism as she turned to face him. "I mean, this is in the list of rules? It says somewhere, 'The fool who followed you up the side of Mt. Everest gets to soap you and scrub you and keep track of your rubber ducky.' "

"Or words to that effect," he said, his voice dry. "By bathing me, you acknowledge my importance. It not only shows that you know where your help is coming from, it indicates your willingness to obey my commands. You will be humbling yourself before an Earth Father."

He pulled his shirt over his head in one fluid movement. "I'm going to get undressed here. You can go behind those rocks or stay here, whatever you want."

As his fingers went to the button fly of his jeans, Laken scooted quickly behind the rocks and began to change into the simple black maillot he had provided. After she had finished, she waited a few minutes more, just in case he was a slow dresser.

When she finally inched her way out from behind the rocks, Marcus was already in the water. Only his chest showed as he leaned back against the side, his eyes closed. Beside the cloverleaf depression was a white towel.

Laken stood for a moment, scratching her chin. In the past three days, every time she had seen that towel it had been draped around his naked hips. Naked. That was fact number one. Fact number two was the way he hadn't said anything about changing his clothes. He said he would get undressed. Naked?

Swallowing heavily, she moved cautiously closer. When she stood at the edge, she glanced quickly downward then away again. Releasing a small sigh of relief, she returned her gaze to him. Through the clear water she could see black swim trunks.

"Here's the soap."

Startled out of her reverie, she took an awkward step backward. His eyes were still closed, but he had raised one hand to hold up a bar of soap.

She cleared her throat and moved back to the edge. Reaching down, she took the soap from him. "What about pollution? Lizards and . . . and whatever other scaly creatures live in these rocks probably stop by here to knock back a couple of quick ones with the guys before they go home to the wife and kids. Won't this stuff—"

"I'm sure all the scaly creatures appreciate your concern," he said, his voice dry, "but the soap is made from the same kind of plant my ancestors used when they bathed. It won't harm them. Stop stalling."

"Right," she muttered as she eased one foot down into the sun-warmed water. "Bath time."

When he shifted his position, she jumped skittishly, but he was simply turning his back to her, indicating, she supposed, that this was where she was to begin.

"If you want me to play medicine man," he said, his voice quiet and smooth, "you have to follow the rules."

She stood where she was for a moment longer then moved her shoulders in a small shrug and knelt behind him. Dipping the soap into the water, she rubbed the bar between her hands. Although it didn't make much lather, the smooth, creamy texture was rather pleasant.

When she could put it off no longer, she reached out and gingerly began to rub her hands over the broad expanse of his back, reminding herself that she had done the same for C.J. when he was little. Although there was obviously more territory to cover, it was sort of the same thing.

It wasn't even close, she admitted a moment later as her pulse picked up its pace and a deep flush spread through her body.

"According to legend—"

Laken dropped the soap and bit her tongue to keep from squeaking as his voice reached her.

"—the Old Ones, the ones we call Earth Fathers, were all from separate tribes. Each was born with the knowledge that he was different, that he had a special connection with the earth. And each knew he wasn't alone. When the time was right, they went out to search for each other. And only when they came together did they understand what they had been born to do. They understood that they were to isolate themselves from the world in order that they might hear the gods speak."

His voice mesmerized her, holding her in thrall as he told of the ancient ones. It was a complex legend, containing tales within tales. They were stories of marvelous adventures. Struggles and achievements. Triumphs and defeats.

"It took more than thirty years," he told her. "They had lost more than half their number and the ones who were left were all old men. But at last it happened. They came face-to-face with the gods. Because of the hardships they had endured and the truths they had discovered, they didn't cower in fear. Each knew he had been tested and found worthy. They stood straight and tall on a hilltop, their faces turned toward the heavens. And at last they came to know the minds of the gods."

It was only as he finished that Laken realized

what he had done. He had used her own trick on her. He had told her the story of the Earth Fathers to help her relax.

"I think you've done enough work on that spot," he said now. "I used to have skin back there."

Muttering an apology, she moved around him until she was kneeling between his thighs.

For a moment she didn't move. She felt as though she needed to regain her equilibrium, as though any sudden movement would cause her to fall.

When she finally found the courage to meet his eyes, Laken found him watching her, studying her face, his gaze lingering on the mole beside her mouth before moving back to her eyes.

"They're changing color again," he said, his voice a rough whisper of sound.

Laken didn't respond. She couldn't. Her throat had closed, her chest growing tight. Catching her lower lip between her teeth, she reached out to move the soap across his chest then slowly followed it with the palm of her right hand.

Did he know? Did he realize that she wasn't washing him? She was absorbing the feel of him, stealing bits of him through her fingertips, letting his energy pass through her. Placing both palms on his shoulders, she slid her hands slowly down his arms.

Her breathing had grown as erratic as her

heartbeat. Something was about to happen. She didn't know what it was, but anticipation of the unknown event suddenly overwhelmed her and she lost herself in the deep darkness of his gaze as she waited for it to happen.

Nothing happened.

A frown twitched at Laken's lips as the electricity that had built to an incredible degree simply disappeared. She didn't know how it was shut off or even who shut it off, but suddenly something that had been there a moment earlier was there no longer.

Leaning to the side, she picked up the bar of soap and began to bathe him again.

"That was well done," he said a few minutes later.

"We're through?"

After a slight pause he said, "This step is complete."

As they made their way down to camp Laken stayed well behind him. She had some heavy thinking to do about whatever it was that almost, but didn't quite, happen.

She tried to tell herself that it didn't happen because she was strong enough and adult enough to remember that Marcus Reed was a cynic, capable of using women, capable of using *her*, as a temporary diversion.

But, of course, it was a lie. What she had felt while she was lost in the bottomless pit of his gaze was stronger than anything she had ever felt before. If the something that almost-but-didn't-quite-happen had actually happened, she would have been pulled under before she even knew it was happening.

Nothing happened because Marcus didn't let it happen.

That night, as they sat on either side of the campfire, neither spoke. The sleeping bags were spread out behind them, but neither made a move to turn in. Occasionally their eyes met across the flickering campfire and sensual tension moved between them in almost visible waves.

When she could stand no more, Laken cleared her throat and sat up straighter.

"Why did Mrs. Curtis and your grandfather never marry?"

He dropped his gaze to his coffee cup. "Two reasons. The first was prejudice. The people in town would have held it against her. The second was prejudice as well. He didn't think any white woman would be strong enough to adjust to his way of life."

"That's really sad. Really . . ." She frowned. "Really stupid. He should have at least asked her. From what I saw, Anabelle Curtis could handle just about anything." She gave an inelegant snort of contempt. "What a chauvinist. No wonder you—" Breaking off just in time, she cleared her throat and changed the subject. "When you were with him, what did you do about religion?"

He smiled. "If you mean, does being Comanche mean I had to turn my back on traditional Judeo-Christian beliefs, the answer is no."

"You just believe both?"

He glanced away from the fire, into the darkness. "I don't believe anything," he said slowly, "but back when I did, I found no conflict. God is God. Comanche religion is closely tied to the earth, respecting all forms of life as well as the planet we live on." He paused. "Jesus Christ came to give a message that was pretty simple. It was about love and respect. The object of the message was humanity. Love and respect your fellowman. If He came back today, I have a feeling there would be more to it. I think He would say, 'Get a clue, people. Look around you. Look at what you're doing to the freaking planet. What are you doing to your children's birthright?' "

Keeping her gaze on his harsh features, Laken let out a slow whistle. "There was actually some feeling in your voice. You care about something."

"No, I don't." The words were tight with annoyance. "I was just saying if I cared, that's what I would care about."

Although Laken knew she should leave it alone, something spurred her on. "Back when you cared and believed, what was your life like? Was Joseph Two Trees as controlled, as . . . limited in emotions as you are?"

"Limited?" he repeated softly.

When he turned his head slowly to look at her, one brow raised, she knew he was reminding her of what almost but didn't quite happen between them up in the hills.

But Laken wasn't going to back down. Keeping her gaze steady, she nodded. "That's what I said. Limited."

His lips curved in a slow, self-mocking smile. "You're right. I am limited. My grandfather was not. He was a warm, openhearted man. At one time I thought he was strong enough to overcome anything. I saw him survive in the wilderness using nothing more than his brains and bare hands, he was that strong, that disciplined. But the modern world fights a different fight. The lawyers defeated him."

There was nothing in his voice now. No pain. No regret. No sadness. Nothing. And it was the loneliest nothing Laken had ever heard.

A cautious person would have, at this point, kept her mouth shut and left well enough alone. Luckily Laken had never considered caution a virtue.

"I've read a little about vision quests." She picked up the coffeepot and poured herself an extra half a cup. "Did your grandfather make you do that?"

He shot a look of irritation in her direction. "My grandfather didn't make me do anything. He told me what I had to do in order to be a man. Whether I chose to do it or not was up to me."

"So you did go on a quest?"

"Yes, I went."

As silence fell between them, she leaned forward, staring at him across the fire, examining his taut features. "You saw something, didn't you?" she said finally. "You really had a vision."

Annoyance had moved smoothly into open displeasure, but once again he answered her question. "Back then I believed," he said. "I thought I had a vision, that the way had been made clear for me by the gods. Now I can see that it was the result of my physical state. Dehydration, starvation, and lack of sleep. It was a hallucination. A waking nightmare." He shook his head. "Something."

"What did you see?"

"I stood on a plateau fifty miles from anything alive." As he spoke he stared into the fire, as though, in the flickering flames, he saw the past. "It was hot. Bright daylight. Then suddenly, within the blink of an eye, it was night. I was naked. And I was in the sky. I wasn't floating or flying or levitating. I was walking. I felt the sky under my feet as solid as the earth. It was midnight blue and crowded with stars. As I moved, the stars moved as well. Glittering points of light gathered close around me and began to settle in my outspread hands. The stars spoke to me. They taught me a song. And as I sang their light spread from my hands to illuminate the whole Comanche nation. Past, present, and future.

"I sang to people in the settlement near De-

Witt and to Comanches on the reservation in Oklahoma and to others scattered all over the world. Their ancestors and descendants—my ancestors and descendants—stood among them, all listening to my song."

He drew in a slow breath. "These were my people, but in my vision, I stood separate from them. I was of them, but not with them." He frowned. "That bothered me. It bothered me quite a lot. I wanted to join them. I wanted to be listening to the song instead of singing it. I didn't want to walk among the stars, I wanted to stand on earth and feel the stars' light shining on me."

He gave a short laugh and shook his head. "But you can't change a vision. It is what it is. I became the One Who Walks with Stars. Starwalker."

Rising abruptly to his feet, he poured his coffee on the fire. "You have to remember I was eleven. The name didn't please me. I wanted something macho. Snarling Bear or Stands with a Bloody Fist." His lips twisted in a self-mocking smile. "Mark Starwalker sounds like someone who should be hanging out with Chewbacca and Obi-Wan Kenobi."

He met her eyes. "So now you know my Comanche name."

With that he dropped his coffee cup and walked briskly away from the fire, into the deep shadows of night.

For a long time Laken simply stared at the spot where he had disappeared.

Marcus Aurelius Starwalker Reed.

He thought he was so controlled, detached from human emotion. Laken knew better. A moment earlier, as he talked to her of his past, she had seen a glimpse of the same torment that had been in his eyes when he was twelve years old.

Wrapping her arms around her waist, she fought the need to go to him. To follow him into the shadows and hold him in her arms until the pain of the past left him.

And it was at that moment that truth struck her like the proverbial bolt of lightning. She loved Marcus.

She loved him.

Giving a shaky little laugh, she ran a hand across her face. Sweet heaven, she loved him.

In the past two weeks Laken had come to know who and what this man was, so where was the dismay? Where was the biting anticipation of pain?

There was none. There was only joy. Joy so enormous, so all-encompassing, it brought tears to her eyes.

He was a man who had made himself as cold and hard as the hills behind her. And she loved him.

Marcus stood in the darkness, every muscle in his body taut with something very close to anger. Dammit, she was getting to him. It wasn't just the interminable prying into his past. It was *her*, just the fact that she was there, near him, making him feel things that he didn't know how to deal with.

He had known in Chicago that Laken was like no one he had ever met, but what he hadn't known was that she had the ability to make him doubt his most staunchly held beliefs.

Now, standing in the darkness, he remembered how he had felt when her hands moved over his body. He remembered how close he had come to pulling her into his arms and making love to her right there on the hillside. Too close. Much too close.

A long time ago Marcus had discovered his own nature. It was written. Set in stone. He couldn't let her, a woman whose role in his life was destined to be minor and of short duration, throw him back to the days when nothing was certain, nothing was clear.

Earlier today, as he stood on a ledge and looked down at the world, he thought he had found some measure of peace. For a while it seemed as though his mind had been set free. Now he saw that it was a false peace, sent to taunt him with dreams of the impossible. And it was somehow tied to Laken. It somehow tied *him* to Laken.

He had to stop this before it went any further.

He had to reach that place deep inside him where his subconscious self lived and convince himself once and for all that Laken Murphy was just another woman.

Because the one unshakable and immutable fact of his life was that Marcus could be tied to no one.

The next morning Laken had barely managed to clean their breakfast dishes when Marcus changed into the black swim trunks and said, "It's your turn."

"My turn?"

He nodded. "Today I bathe you."

She frowned. "I thought you were supposed to be the important one. I'm just the handmaiden. Subservient and all that."

"That's right," he said slowly, watching her face. "But this part of the ritual shows that the shaman is of the earth. Mortal. It illustrates my connection to humanity."

Taking the black swimsuit off the rocks where she had hung it to dry the day before, he handed it to her then turned away from the camp.

Following reluctantly, she called, "Hey, wait. . . . Listen, Marcus, I just thought of something. Since this is a symbolic kind of thing, we could probably . . . oh, I don't know, we could probably do something like spit on our hands and shake and agree that you're mortal. Something like that," she finished hopefully.

When he glanced back at her, his dark eyes glittered with something that looked suspiciously like mischief. "I don't think so. As participants, we have to experience each step to prepare us for the final stage. Think of it as hiring someone to do a job for you, like adding a room onto your house. The carpenter doesn't spit on his hand and shake and agree that he's cut the wood to the right length. He has to actually cut it. If he doesn't complete each step, the end product will be a big mess."

"Sure, I can see that," she murmured.

Laken understood what he was saying. She really did. But the thought of him bathing her had brought a kaleidoscope of visions. And each one added to the heat in her flushed cheeks. Loving him was one thing. Letting him see how vulnerable she was to his touch was something else.

"I can see that," she repeated slowly.

Glancing around, she realized that rather than going uphill, they were climbing down the slope toward the creek.

"How come we're going down here?" she asked. "Don't I get to use the little clover bathtub?"

"No," he said, "you don't."

As they walked along the near side of the stream, they passed the place where she cleaned the utensils and they passed the place where he had cut the willow limbs. At times the ravine was cluttered with broken boulders and the going was almost as rough as the uphill climb had been.

At last he stopped walking and, as he had the day before, said, "This is it."

Laken glanced around. Downstream from where they stood, the ravine took a sharp turn to the left. On the other side of the narrow stream, immediately across from them, a cottonwood tree that was still green and healthy even though its roots were exposed, made a natural bridge across the water.

Looking down into the water, Laken saw her reflection as well as that of the cottonwood. Below the reflections, she saw smooth rocks and gravel.

Turning her head, she examined the area immediately around them. At one time the stream had been wider at the bend, and when the water receded, it left behind an expanse of shiny mud that was now separated from the stream by a line of boulders.

Frowning, Laken glanced over her shoulder at Marcus. "Okay, I give. I don't see anything here that's different from any other spot on the stream."

"Don't you?" He took a couple of steps forward.

"Careful," she warned, "you're headed for the mud bog."

"Yes, I know. This is it."

"What's it?"

"This is the next step." He nodded toward the lagoon of mud.

She stared at the mud for a moment then cut her eyes back toward him. "What are we going to do, make adobe?"

"My ancestors didn't use adobe." He paused, his lips twitching in a smile. "You'd better change."

"Hold on. I need a little information here. Why—"

"The next part of the ritual begins here," he interrupted and once again he nodded toward the mud.

Laken was not liking the sound of this. Nor did she like the look in his eyes. "The next part of the ritual begins at a mud hole," she said slowly.

"In order to differentiate between the subservient handmaiden, to use your own words, and the Earth Father, you have to have a coat of mud on you before I bathe you."

She took a hasty step backward, away from him and away from the gleaming mud. "You're saying that to tell the difference between nobody —that would be me—and somebody—that would be you—I have to roll around in the mud?"

He shrugged. "I don't make this stuff up. You wanted me to use the ancient ways. This is just another part of the whole process." He paused, his expression innocent, almost pleasant, as he regarded her. "If you have some objection, we can always call the whole thing off. But if we're going to continue, you have to stop questioning the ways of the Earth Fathers."

Laken stared at him for a long moment, her eyes narrowed, then she swung around and walked behind a clump of low-growing willows. She changed into the swimsuit, flinging her clothes around in a temper as she cursed him and all his ancestors.

When she finally walked out from behind the trees, adjusting the straps and the fit around her legs as she moved, she was still muttering under her breath.

She stopped beside him and raised her chin. "I'm going to do this, but I have to tell you, if I were one of those old guys, after waiting years and years, losing half my friends not to mention some important body parts along the way, and the gods finally showed up and told me the truth has something to do with *mud* . . . Well, I can tell you, I would be pretty darn ticked."

Her nostrils flared as she took in his expression. "And don't you dare nod at that stupid mud hole again. I know damn well what I have to do."

He was laughing. He wasn't laughing aloud, but Laken knew without a doubt that inside he was laughing himself silly.

Holding her breath, she stepped into the mud and immediately sank up to her ankles. After taking several slurping steps out into the mess, she drew in a deep breath, closed her eyes, and sat down.

A second later a low moan escaped her as she sank down in the warm ooze.

He was laughing openly now. When Laken heard him, she opened one eye and gave him half a glare. "Do you have any idea what this feels like? Have you ever had to do it?"

"I'm the shaman," he said, still laughing. "Medicine men don't roll around in the mud."

"I see." Laken's voice was quite steady. And her movements were just as steady when she picked up a handful of mud and slung it in his direction.

He stopped laughing. For a moment he simply stood on the edge of the mire and gazed down at the glop of mud that was slowly sliding down his bare chest.

Now it was Laken's turn to laugh. "Mr. Earth Father," she taunted in an unsteady voice. "Mr. Comanche warrior. Mr. high-and-mighty shaman. Now who's—"

She broke off abruptly when she caught a glimpse of what was in his dark eyes. As she watched he bent down and scooped up a handful of mud.

Although she couldn't manage to stop laughing, when he raised his hand she began to scoot backward. "No . . . listen . . . wait, Marcus—no . . . *no*—"

She was still saying no when the warm, slick

stuff hit the side of her face. Amusement died as she drew in a deep, slow breath.

"I guess you know," she said quietly, "this means war." Instantly she was on her knees, slinging mud with both hands.

He stepped into the bog, dodging the barrage of missiles, returning her fire as he made his way toward her.

Ducking to the side, he grabbed at her hands to halt the latest onslaught—and lost his balance. Laken responded with a burst of laughter that continued even when her knees slipped out from under her, landing her in the mud beside him. And then they were holding on to each other, rolling from side to side, laughing like fools.

"Mr. hot-shot architect," she said, her voice breathless. "The King of Cool."

Her head was resting on his shoulder and they were covered with mud, from the tops of their heads to the bottom of their feet.

"Miss A-I Auto Parts," he returned. "Trouble with a capital *T*. We make quite a pair."

Picking up her right hand, he began slowly to slide his fingers in and out from between hers.

Laken couldn't have been more shocked if he had suddenly decided to stand on his head. He was concentrating all his attention on their joined hands, exploring each finger, savoring them, as though he had never felt a hand like this or known fingers like these existed.

Swallowing with difficulty, Laken stared up at

him, her eyes wide, her pulse rapid, as he smoothed his hands up her arms and across her shoulders, over her neck and the tops of her breasts.

And then, without a pause to allow her to adjust to the change, he stood up and helped her to her feet.

Giving him a sideways glance, she said with an awkward smile, "I had forgotten how mud itches when it starts to dry on your body."

Although he returned her smile, he made no response. Still holding her hand, he led her across to the opposite side of the bog and on around the bend in the stream.

A moment later Laken caught her breath in surprise. "It's a page out of a fairy tale," she said, her voice filled with awe as she stared at the little waterfall that splashed into a rock-lined pool.

"No, it's real," he told her as they stepped into the stream.

For the past few days Laken had washed dishes in this stream and knew the water was ice-cold. But now, against the heat of her body, it didn't even feel cool.

When they reached the pool they swam, moving through the water to wash away the mud. Then, catching her hand, he climbed up to a layer of rocks above the pool and they stood together beneath the gently splashing water of the fall.

"Now it's my turn," he told her.

Immediately he began to smooth his hands over her body, keeping his gaze steadily on her face.

There was something strange in those dark eyes, she told herself. Something strange . . . and a little frightening. It was almost as though he were gauging her reaction, analyzing the effect he was having on her.

Laken fought against the effects of his touch. She knew him. She would be worse than foolish if she let this happen.

A moment later, when she felt his fingers in her hair gently moving on her scalp and out to the ends, causing a shiver of pleasure to work its way through her body, she had to give in to the fact that she was worse than foolish.

Closing her eyes, she let the feeling flood over her. She not only allowed it, she reveled in it. She joyously gave herself over to it.

"I can't get it all unless I take off the suit."

The sound of his husky voice brought her eyes open slightly. He wasn't waiting for permission. Already his hands were moving on her shoulders, sliding the narrow black straps down her arms.

And still he watched. His dark gaze never strayed from her face as he spread his fingers across the tops of her breasts and pushed the suit slowly down, exposing her breasts.

Only then did he stop studying her face. Lowering his head, he examined the white flesh of her breasts, the dark tips as tight and hard as the water-polished pebbles in the stream.

A rough sound of pleasure caught in his throat and he raised his head to look at her. Deep grooves of bewilderment spread across his brow and he gave his head one short shake.

"This is not how it's supposed to be," he said in a harsh whisper. "Dammit, it's not supposed to be like this."

Groaning, he leaned down and took one dark nipple into his mouth, sucking hard as though he needed it desperately and couldn't get enough.

A breathy little moan escaped Laken and then she was reaching out to him, pulling his head closer.

As he moved from one breast to the other, Laken's hands slid down the sides of his neck to his shoulders. She knew this body now. Yesterday, when she bathed him, she had claimed it with her hands. And last night she had claimed it with her heart. She recognized each curve, each hard muscle. And for this moment they belonged to her.

As he pushed the bathing suit lower his mouth moved lower as well. Dropping to his knees, he raised his hands to the backs of her legs, moving her, rearranging her with a gentle but firm touch.

An instant later, when she felt his mouth on her, there at the center, she threw her head back and drew in a deep breath as pleasure, more intense than anything she had ever known, spread through her in waves that grew more urgent with each passing moment.

Her fingers curled into his shoulders, and for the next few minutes there was nothing in her world except his hot mouth and the cool water.

When the climax rocked through her, a high-pitched cry came from deep inside her, and if he hadn't moved, if he hadn't stood up to catch her close to him, she would have fallen.

As her strength returned she found to her surprise that the aftereffects of being loved by Marcus were almost as potent as the event itself.

With a warm rush of emotion, she moved against the hard body that was still pressed close to hers. She wasn't ready for it to be over. Moving her body against his, she spread urgent kisses across his shoulder, his neck and his chest. She let her lips drift down his body, this amazing body that for a while belonged to her.

When he framed her face with his hands and brought her up straight, she moaned in disappointment and held up a hand to stop the soft kisses he was brushing across her lips.

"Don't stop me," she whispered as her gaze searched his face. "I want this. I want you to feel what I felt. I want to hold your pleasure in my fingers and my mouth."

He shook his head. "No, not now," he murmured. "We've had enough for today."

Reaching up, he brushed a strand of damp

hair from her cheek. Even though the movement was tender, something had changed. A chill that had nothing to do with the icy water was filtering through her skin.

He was shutting her out. He was deliberately taking himself out of her reach.

A little shaft of pain struck, and she dipped her head, tearing her gaze from his face. Scooping up the bathing suit, she stepped out of the water and pulled it on.

As she shook the water from her hair she sensed that he was watching her again. Turning her head, she met his eyes.

And then she knew. Once again, without knowing how she knew, she understood what was going on in his mind. She knew why he had shut her out.

Moments earlier, when he gave her such intense pleasure, she had been completely vulnerable. And he had been in complete control. There was no way he was going to allow their positions to be reversed.

This was Marcus Aurelius Starwalker Reed, a man who had fought all his life to be vulnerable to no one.

NINE

When she had finished rinsing out the coffeepot, Laken sat down on the rocks beside the stream. Although it wasn't yet hot, the sun was bright, reflecting in the water, bouncing off the polished rocks on the bank.

If one wanted to get technical, what she was doing could probably be called dawdling. The plain fact was, Laken didn't want to go back to camp until she had done some heavy thinking.

Judging by the tension that had existed between her and Marcus last night and again this morning, she needed to take a hard look at reality.

The first piece of reality was the fact that she loved him. Something in this man who made a career of closing himself off to the world had reached a part of her that no one else had ever reached. She was totally, completely, wholeheartedly given over to loving him.

The second was the fact that he didn't return her love. This bit of truth brought a deep, abiding pain that she was afraid might be permanent, but that didn't make it any less the truth.

And then she tackled the third piece of reality. What she felt and what Marcus didn't feel had to take a backseat until C.J. was well again. Laken couldn't allow either of them to get sidetracked. They had to do what they came here to do.

It was a ticklish situation. If the scene at the waterfall hadn't taken place, she could have pretended that everything was the same as it had been before. She could go around hiding the fact that she loved him, and he could go around being annoyed with her and life in general. But it had taken place. It was there between them, as solid as a brick wall.

Laken was the kind of person who walked up to a problem—chased it down if necessary—grabbed it by the collar, and said, "Okay, here's the deal."

But her way was not Marcus's way. Judging by his attitude, his way was to stare up at the hills while he mentally put more bricks in the wall.

When, a moment later, she heard his footsteps on the gravel, Laken metaphorically girded her loins and glanced up.

"We need a break," he said without meeting her gaze.

Raising one arched brow, she got to her feet. "We do?"

"Let me rephrase that." He paused to push restless fingers through his dark hair. "I need a break. A friend of mine, the friend I borrowed the Jeep from, has a ranch about a hundred and fifty miles from here. Leon Gajducek. You've probably heard of him." He cut his eyes toward her and took in her blank expression. "Maybe not. A couple of times a year he invites two or three hundred people to come for the weekend. The best of the best," he said, his voice scornful.

The brick wall was complete and they were suddenly back to square one. Marcus looked and sounded like the bored cynic she had found on entering his office that first day.

Exhaling a small sigh, Laken scratched the tip of her nose. "That sounds . . . nice. The thing is, I generally give the go-by to parties attended by people who call themselves 'the best of the best.' It's not that I'm prejudiced or anything, I simply prefer—"

"Covered-dish dinners?"

The undisguised mockery in his voice caused her lips to tighten, but she simply nodded. "That's right. So why don't you drop me off at that little motel behind the trading post and I'll wait there for you."

"I don't think so." Although he kept his tone even, suppressed anger began to gleam in his deep-set eyes. "Do I have to remind you that you need me? The medicine man runs the show."

"You know, that excuse is getting a little old," she yelled at his back as he walked away.

When she reached the Jeep, it was packed. The motor was running and he sat behind the wheel. Throwing the breakfast things into the back, she climbed in beside him and slammed the door.

As he rammed the gearshift into first and stepped hard on the gas, throwing Laken's head back, she decided that if she went at it with absolute dedication, she might just be able to work this love thing out of her system.

The first hundred miles passed in silence as he used anger, unfounded anger, to hold himself at a distance.

Typical, she told herself. A clean, honest explosion was too low-class for Mr. God Almighty Reed. Too human.

"Look," she said finally, "if I'm going to this shindig, don't you think you'd better fill in a few details? What kind of entertainment does your friend usually lay on? Are we talking about watching the cowhands twirl their branding irons or should I call Rose and tell her to FedEx my tiara?"

Without taking his gaze from the dusty road, he said, "Leon is an artist. His work was famous in the fifties. He hasn't painted in years, but he keeps his hand in by helping promising newcomers and offering his home as a retreat. Once a year he invites a few friends and a lot of people who are prominent in the art world to come out for the weekend. On the first night, everyone gets together for a viewing his protégés' work. Food, drink, mixing, and mingling. He usually brings in a small orchestra for dancing on the terrace. That kind of thing."

She studied his face for a moment. " 'That kind of thing' sounds suspiciously like a party, which means clothes, which in case you haven't noticed, I haven't got any of at the moment."

He shrugged. "Brady, the nearest town, is small, but because of the crowd Leon pulls in, the shops are geared for the elite."

"Sounds dandy," she muttered.

As he had told her, Brady was small. But every building, every house, was a shining example of the picturesque. It was a make-believe town, catering to make-believe people.

They drove through town and stopped in front of a hotel that had the haughty look of a turn-of-the-century mansion. After booking two rooms, Marcus left her on her own to cope with the curious stares from the people in the lobby and the man who carried her grungy little bag up to her room.

Laken barely glanced at the elegant bedroom. She went straight through to the bathroom and began to run water in the claw-footed tub, dumping in half a bottle of the lavender-scented bubble bath provided by the hotel.

To hell with Marcus Aurelius Starwalker

Reed, she told herself as she sank down in the warm water. If he thought she was going to tremble in the face of his stupid moods, he had another think coming.

The bath worked miracles, soothing away the rough edges on her nerves, and an hour later, when she heard a knock at the door, Laken was feeling almost mellow.

She pulled on a thick white bathrobe, also provided by the hotel, and continued to dry her hair as she walked to the door.

As soon as she opened it, she found a stack of boxes being shoved into her arms.

"Here," Marcus said brusquely. "Now you can stop complaining."

She glanced at the boxes then back to him. "What's all this?"

He didn't answer. He was staring, one hand still raised in a frozen gesture, at her hair, at the damp, shining curls that fell down her back and across her shoulders.

After a moment he lowered his hand, cleared his throat, and nodded toward the white boxes. "Open them."

Placing the boxes on the bed, she untied the string on the largest one. Inside, under layers of pink tissue paper, was an emerald-green satin dress. Reaching into the folds, Laken found the price tag and instantly caught her breath in shock.

He had followed her to the bed. Now, reaching out, he took the dress out of her hands and held it up to her, pulling a handful of auburn curls over her shoulder so that they fell across the green satin.

"Watch out," she said, pushing the dress away. "If you get water stains on it, they won't take it back."

He stared at her, his brow creasing in confusion. "Why should they take it back? Is it the wrong size?"

"No, it's exactly the right size and I'm not sure what that says about your experience with women," she said, her voice dry. "But you'll still have to take it back. I can't afford it."

Pulling the dress out of his hands, she began to fold it when it was suddenly jerked out of her hands.

"It's a gift," he said tightly, and threw it across the bed. "The freaking dress is a gift."

With a smile twitching at her lips, she shook her head. "Sorry. I can't accept it. You can keep it if you want. It's not your size and I'm not sure how that shade of green would look on you, but it's your choice. I'll take care of my clothes on my own."

He ran a hand across his face and glanced away from her. "You're acting like a fool." The words were low and tight. "The expense incurred for this weekend doesn't have anything to do with the other thing. Coming here was my idea, so there is no way your plebeian sense of morals or integrity or whatever could be offended. Be ready at seven, and by God"—his voice had risen, his dark eyes blazing with renewed anger—"you'd better be wearing that *son-of-a-bitching dress!*"

When he swung around on his heels and walked out of the room, slamming the door behind him, Laken's eyebrows went up in surprise.

It might be her imagination, but it seemed to her that old Granite Heart was loosening up just a tad.

At exactly seven o'clock, just as she was applying a layer of cinnamon lipstick, he returned. Grabbing a stole from the back of a chair, she walked to the door and opened it.

He had changed into a dark dinner jacket and looked smooth and handsome. Polished and slightly aristocratic. As far away from the man she had spent the past few days with as it was possible to get.

Once again, his gaze went first to her hair. Tonight although she wore it up, Laken had made no attempt to suppress the curls. Instead she let them have their way and provide a frame for her face.

His gaze moved from her hair to her face, lingering on the mole beside her mouth.

When she felt her lips tingle in automatic response, Laken cleared her throat. "I'm ready," she said.

And that was when he finally noticed what she was wearing.

She had been lucky to find the white chiffon halter dress. The fabric was good, the cut excellent, and the price drastically cut for an end-of-the-season sale. Even at the peak of the season, though, the dress had never been as expensive as the green satin. It was a dress Laken could afford to buy for herself.

Although she had expected another outburst from him, had almost looked forward to it, there was nothing. No outrage. No barely suppressed anger. Instead, after glancing briefly at the flesh that filled in the low-cut V-neckline, he dropped his gaze to the gold bracelets on her wrist.

A smile that she could have sworn was involuntary curved his lips. "Think you'll need luck tonight?"

She raised one arched brow. "Don't you?"

She thought for a moment that he was actually going to respond, but then his smile faded, he took her arm, and they left the room.

It was still light when they drove under the white arch at the entrance to his friend's ranch. After a mile or so, the Jeep topped a rise and she saw the red tile roof of the main house. It was square and had been built around a palm-lined swimming pool. Set apart from the house was a structure that might once have been a barn. Now it was mostly glass, three stories high, gleaming gold in the light from the setting sun.

Passing the house, they drove toward the glass building. Cars were parked edge to edge in the gravel parking lot and the adjoining field. As he stopped before the double doors one uniformed valet opened the passenger door while another took the key from Marcus.

As he joined her at the door she whispered, "I should have brought my camera."

He might have chuckled then. She couldn't be sure.

Inside the door, Laken stopped and blinked several times, trying to take in the accumulated glitz. There were hundreds of people, holding champagne glasses, talking and laughing.

Earlier, as she dressed, Laken had given some thought to the coming evening, so she wasn't surprised when Marcus turned to her and said, "I see some friends. Will you be all right by yourself for a few minutes?"

"Go for it. I'm fine."

His eyes narrowed as he examined her features. A moment later he turned and walked away.

He had expected her to be insulted or at the very least shaken by his desertion. Her easy compliance confused him. Good. It would give him something to think about.

Grabbing a glass from a passing waiter, she began to make her way toward the center of the massive room, where a half wall split the area. This was where the paintings were displayed.

Stopping in front of one, she sipped her wine and gave the painting her full attention. The background was a pleasant if distorted landscape. In the foreground were misshapen figures, their hair and bodies depicted in colors that couldn't have existed in reality. Most of the faces were contorted with laughter, but Laken's gaze kept returning to one figure. A small figure, almost lost in the laughing crowd. There was no laughter here. The dark, outsized eyes held something that made her take an awkward step back.

"You can't stop looking at it, can you?"

Turning her head, Laken found a man standing beside her. He was tall and thin with iron-gray hair that he wore pulled back tightly in a ponytail. Although everyone else in the room was dressed formally, this man wore a black T-shirt with black jeans. There was something a little decadent about his ferret-sharp features, something that reminded her of the sort of people who had made their way to Germany during the wild days before World War II.

Although he was watching her with a pleasant smile, Laken had the distinct feeling this man could be more than a little malicious when he chose.

With an answering smile, she returned her gaze to the painting. "No, you're right. I want to stop looking at it, but I can't. There's something compulsive in there. Compulsive and disturbing."

"So you don't like it?"

"It's not a matter of liking. Liking is for a little girl with a rose against her cheek, which is what I have on my bedroom wall, or people skating on a frozen pond, which is what's hanging over my couch. This is something else. Instead of making you smile when you look at it, it gives you a little pain right here." She pressed a hand to her chest. "I would not have this in my house," she said, underscoring each word.

"You sound very definite about that." He paused. "You wouldn't have it in your house because of that little pain?"

Reaching up to scratch the tip of her nose, she gathered her thoughts. "Yes, but that's not the whole reason. You see, at first you would be caught by it every time you passed, and it would give you a jolt. But after a while you would get used to it. It would become part of the surroundings, like the ugly ceramic figurine you have to keep out because your boss's wife gave it to you and you never know when she'll drop by." She glanced at him. "And that would be criminal. I mean, the fact that it would lose its impact on you. You *should* feel something when you look at it. It's important that you feel something." She smiled and her shoulders twitched in a slight shrug. "Does that make sense?"

"Interesting," he murmured, still studying her face. "You're not the first person I've asked about this particular painting, but you're the first who's given me anything other than a stock answer filled with art-world catchphrases."

"That means my answer was good?"

He nodded. "Very good."

"So what do I win?"

Chuckling, he took her arm and moved with her to the next painting. "You win a chance to tell me about this one."

Laken turned to look at the painting. It was enormous, filling most of the wall. The background was sunshine yellow and squarely in the center was a plate of food. Fried eggs, a thick slice of ham, and two golden-brown biscuits. As she stared at it Laken's stomach rumbled in protest.

The man beside her glanced at her, one gray brow raised. "An astute observation, darling. It is indeed realistic. And if I can hear your stomach growling over this noise, you need food immediately."

"Real food?" she asked hopefully. "I caught a glimpse of what's on those silver trays and we'd have to cop half a dozen of them to do me any good."

"Real food," he said, taking her arm again to guide her across the room.

Half an hour later they were in a small kitchen off the main room. Laken's ponytailed knight errant sat on the corner of the small wooden table, watching as she finished a plate of scrambled eggs, bacon, and toast.

Exhaling a sigh filled with contentment, she raised her gaze to his face. "I suppose you know if you had offered me strawberry jam instead of grape jelly, I would have traded my body for this meal."

He grinned. "I suppose you know if I weren't gay, I would now be searching desperately for a jar of strawberry jam."

Laughing, she wiped her mouth with a checked napkin and leaned back in the chair. "So here's what I know about you. I know you're intelligent and that you have good taste in women even if you don't want to bed them. What I don't know is your name. I have a feeling you might be my host. Leon Something with a *chek* on the end."

"Leon Gajducek. That's me. And you're the lovely lady who walked in with the stunning Marcus Aurelius and was immediately deserted by him."

"Laken Murphy. That's me." She studied him for a moment. "You're not after him, are you? I hope not, because I have to tell you, I don't think I've ever met a man more solidly heterosexual."

He shook his head. "He's a beautiful man, but much too forceful for my tastes."

"Ditto."

He chuckled. "Liar, liar, pants on fire. And here I thought you were that rare thing—an honest woman."

"Apparently we were both fooled," she said, her voice dry. "I didn't take you for a sexist."

"Do you deny the female of the species is dishonest by nature?"

"Absolutely. Nature has nothing to do with it." After smiling at his appreciative burst of laughter, she continued. "All the way back through history, they wrote about deceitful women. What the poets and historians rarely tell you is that because those women lived in societies that found them worthless, they had to use deception to survive."

"Point taken," he said with a nod. "But now you must concede there were those who used deception simply to gain power."

"Sure they did. And how many men have done the same? The difference is, for the most part when women deceive, it's the result of a conscious decision. Men do it without being aware of it. They not only lie to women, they lie to themselves as well."

"Interesting," he murmured, just as he had when he first met her. "So . . . are you going to tell me what's going on between you and the Iceman? Why did he bring you here?"

She shrugged. "Who knows?"

"I think you do. I also think you know that whatever his reason was, it wasn't nice."

She laughed. "No, nice is not a word I would use to describe Marcus. But a man doesn't have to be nice to make you crazy for him."

He sighed. "Ain't it the truth."

When she laughed, he laughed with her and pushed away from the table. "Time to get back. Listen, darling, I would consider it a great honor if you'd allow me to introduce you to some of my friends and acquaintances."

Although Leon's expression was still pleasant, Laken wasn't fooled. He was an extremely polite centurion inviting the poor Christian to get to know the lions a little better.

Marcus slammed his wineglass down on a table in frustration. Dammit, how could he have lost her? For almost an hour he had been looking for Laken and she was nowhere to be found.

Although he had intentionally left her on her own, she was supposed to stay where he could keep an eye on her, damn her. One minute she had been looking at the paintings, the next she was nowhere in sight. He had even checked the parking lot to make sure the Jeep was still there.

Just then, just when he had decided it was time to enlist Leon's help in finding Laken, Marcus spotted her. She was across the room, standing at the center of a group of people. Her eyes, bright blue now, were sparkling with laughter. Leon stood beside her, watching her closely. Too closely. The patent interest in the older man's expression brought a biting twinge of jealousy, a twinge that grew to a sharp stab when he saw that Leon wasn't the only one watching her.

And the other men around her weren't gay.

Jeff Davies, the tall, blond man on Laken's immediate right, owned a string of well-known galleries and had slept with every woman in the room who was under the age of sixty and over the age of consent.

Marcus's lips tightened in anger and he began to move toward her. But before he had taken two steps, Davies leaned over to speak to Laken. With a brilliant smile, she handed her glass to Leon and walked away with Davies.

Skirting the edge of the room, Marcus ignored the people trying to talk to him and made his way out to the terrace. When he reached it, the small orchestra was playing a tango. The other couples had stopped dancing, moving out of the way to watch Laken and Davies.

Marcus's fingers clenched into tight fists at his sides as he watched along with the others. The tango had never seemed as blatantly erotic to him as it did now. The white chiffon dress swirled around her legs. Davies's thighs moved against hers, their bodies sliding together, then away, then together again.

And the whole time her hazel eyes were alive with excitement, her features flushed with pleasure.

Damn her to hell.

The instant the last note faded away, as she was still laughing up at Davies, Marcus was beside them, catching her arm in a tight grasp.

"I think the next one is mine." He heard the abruptness of the words, recognized the undisguised anger in his voice, but there was nothing he could do about it.

Apparently Laken heard as well. There was speculation in her expression as she listened to Davies thank her for the dance then turned back to Marcus.

They stood for a moment facing each other, neither moving. "You dance beautifully," he said finally.

"Don't sound so surprised," she said with a little smile. "The lower classes dance. After my parents died, before I got my finances straightened out, I took a second job as a dance instructor. My looks and personality got me the job, but I wouldn't have kept it if I hadn't been a quick study."

"I want you to tango with me."

She nodded toward the orchestra. "They're playing a waltz."

He pulled her into his arms. "So we'll waltz. Someday we'll tango."

She glanced at him through her lashes. "You make it sound like a threat."

"Maybe that's how I meant it."

It was almost two in the morning when they stopped at the door of Laken's hotel room. After unlocking the door, she hesitated before raising her eyes to his. "It didn't go the way you had it planned, did it?"

"No," he said, his voice curt.

At least he wasn't trying to deny it. "You wanted me to fall flat on my face," she said, exhaling a small sigh. "You wanted me to make a fool of myself in front of your high-class friends."

"That's right. I did."

Running her gaze over his tight, angry features, she said, "Why?"

"I came here to get back to reality. To see you in real terms."

She shook her head. "I don't understand."

He gave a harsh laugh. "No, I don't suppose you do."

An instant later she found herself flattened against the door. Earlier that day she had wished that he would let go of his tightly maintained facade. She was suddenly, explosively, getting her wish.

His hands were shaking as he grasped her neck and found her mouth with his in a kiss that shook her soul.

"I want you," he whispered tightly against her lips. "Do you understand that? Dammit, it's more than just wanting you. It's an obsession. And it's not supposed to be this way. It's not supposed to be something that overtakes me until I can't think of anything else. I brought you here to convince myself that you were ordinary. Just another woman. It was a *lie.*" The words were tight and hoarse as he reached behind her to open the door to her room. "It was a damned lie. Put you in a crowd of a thousand and it would still be the same as it was out there in the hills. I want you until sometimes I think I'm dying of it."

Before she could even try to respond, they were on the bed. Once, as his naked body settled over hers, Laken told herself that she shouldn't be allowing this to happen. She would only get hurt. For her own protection, she should stop it before it went too far.

But it had already gone too far. The instant he began to touch her, she couldn't think of anything but his touch. There was no stopping it. It was as inevitable and unchangeable as the earth revolving around the sun.

When he parted her thighs and moved between them, she was ready, almost as though she had been waiting her whole life for this moment. They were one now. A part of each other. And no matter what happened in the future, nothing would ever change that.

He was no longer holding himself at a distance. His control was gone, leaving him as ripped apart by his need for her as she was by her need for him. He was free in a way she had never seen before. There was nothing studied about the way he moved or the rough sounds he made when she touched him.

When she reached the apex and waves of pleasure began to rock through her, she fought to keep her eyes open so she could see it happen for him. His head was thrown back, the tendons in his neck stretched tight.

The wildness of his climax thrilled her, sending electric waves of pleasure through her all over again.

She had done this for him. For just a little while she had set him free.

When Laken came awake, she was alone in the bed. She glanced around as panic gripped her in an automatic reaction to his absence.

An instant later she saw him standing at the window. As her pulse slowed she watched him, studying the face lit by moonlight. He didn't know she was watching and had let down his guard. It was like looking at the photograph of him at age twelve. Wounded. Vulnerable in his loneliness.

"Why didn't you go to your grandfather's funeral?"

She didn't know where the question came from. She had given it no thought. It had simply come out, fully formed.

When he didn't turn, she thought maybe he hadn't heard her, but after a moment he shifted his position and reached up to brush a hand across his face.

"I found out about his death by accident." The words were slow and quiet. "I heard my aunt and uncle talking about it. Naturally, I confronted them. I had been with them for five years by then. I was seventeen and had learned their rules, but there was still some of the wildness left and I wanted to kill them for trying to keep it from me. I demanded that they let me go back to bury him. Aunt Miriam wouldn't even listen. When I told her—when I let her know I was going, with or without her consent, she had me locked in my bedroom." He paused. "It wasn't easily accomplished."

"I'll bet it wasn't," she murmured. "And pardon me for saying so, but she was a just a little dense to think anything so puny as a locked door would stop you."

"No, it didn't stop me. I climbed out the window. My bedroom was on the third floor, but I had been trained by Joseph Two Trees. I had made rougher climbs. I hitched part of the way and walked the rest. I got to DeWitt three days after the funeral."

Although the words held no inflection, she knew what emotion lay behind them. She could almost feel the old pain settling around him.

"I talked to my cousins at the settlement and made sure the ceremonies due him as a shaman had taken place. I spent a couple of days out on the range, then I gave myself up to the private investigators who had been watching the cemetery since the day after I left Chicago."

She climbed out of the bed and moved to stand behind him, wrapping her arms around him, pushing her body close to his, trying to warm him.

For a moment he held himself stiff, then he turned slowly to face her. Staring into his eyes, she placed a hand on either side of his face and brushed her open mouth softly across his. Once, twice, three times.

"Come back to bed, love," she whispered. "I need you."

A rough sound caught in his throat, and then he was carrying her back to the bed.

The first cold rays of light were trickling through the curtains. Marcus lay in the bed beside Laken, watching her sleeping face. Reaching up, he brushed an auburn curl from her temple.

Come back to bed, love. I need you.

The words echoed in his mind. Last night, when he heard them, something broke loose inside him. He felt things he hadn't felt in years. A flood tide of warmth and pain, love and regret.

It was too much, he told himself now. He had known it last night, but last night he had been too wrapped up in the feel of her to do any rational thinking.

Now, in the hard light of day, he knew what he had to do.

When Laken woke up again, Marcus was pulling on a blue chambray shirt. As though sensing her gaze on him, he turned his head slightly to look at her.

Something in his face, something in those dark, unfathomable eyes, made her catch her breath. "What is it?" she asked, the words unconsciously urgent.

As she watched, his expression changed and he closed her out. "I'm sorry, Laken," he said quietly.

She sat up, pulling the sheet over her breasts. "I don't think I like the sound of that," she said with an awkward little laugh. "What are you apologizing for?"

"For everything. For bringing you here. For that farce up in the hills."

"What—"

"The plan was revenge." He paused to draw in a slow breath. "The whole thing was a lie. A fairy tale I concocted to punish you."

Her first reaction was relief that it wasn't anything more serious. Then, as she understood the full implications of what he was saying, anger took over.

Sliding out of the bed, she gave no notice to the fact that she was naked as she moved closer to him, keeping her eyes on his face.

"You made it up?" she said, her voice uncharacteristically soft. "Bathing you. Rolling in the mud. That *damned mud!* You made it all up?"

He gave one short nod. "All of it. It wasn't only that I wanted to pay you back for—" He broke off and leaned his head back against the window. "After Joe died, I made myself forget. It wasn't easy. It took years. But I did it. It's all gone. Everything he taught me is gone."

"Starwalker?"

He shook his head. "No, that was true. But it's the only thing that was. I'm not your shaman. I can't help C.J. It was a cruel trick. Only now, after getting close to you, do I realize just how cruel it was. If I hadn't come to . . . to like you, I probably would have played the whole thing out. But I did, and I can't."

"You like me," she repeated, her voice dull.

"That shouldn't surprise you. You're an extremely likable person. Ask Leon. Or anyone else you met at the party last night."

"And last night, what happened here—"

A short sound of irritation caught in his throat. "There's nothing mysterious about that. When I see an attractive woman, like most men, I want to sleep with her. Why shouldn't I?"

She moistened her lips, her gaze darting around in confusion. "You mean . . . What you're saying is that, for you, making love is sort of like counting coup. It puts you one up on the other warriors."

"You can't feel any more contempt for me than I do for myself." His voice was rough as he met her eyes. "But I want to make it up to you. If you'll give me a little time, I'm sure I can find someone who can help C.J. Someone who will be able to convince him to let psychiatric therapy work . . . and of course, I'll take care of all the expenses."

She had to turn away from the words, from the look on his face. She was desperately trying to think over the pounding in her head and heart. She had known he didn't believe in anything, not even love. She had told herself over and over again that he did not and would never care for her. But somehow, last night—

She clenched her teeth together, firming her chin. So she had been wrong about last night. Maybe in time she would be able to accept that without feeling that her still-beating heart was being ripped from her body.

Right now she had to think about C.J.

Drawing in a slow breath, she brushed the hair from her cheek with a brisk movement. "Okay . . . okay, I understand what you're saying. Something along the lines of so long and thanks for all the nooky. But it's not going to be that way."

Rage, blessed rage, was pushing the pain aside, leaving her lips tight, her voice harsh. "It is *not.* You promised to help. And I don't mean by spending money and calling in specialists. You promised to play Comanche shaman. You promised." She exhaled a slow, uneven breath. "I'm holding you to that promise."

"Didn't you hear—"

"I heard. It was all fake. Fine. Just keep it up." The words were hard and flat. "You convinced me. Now do the same with C.J. It won't be that difficult. He's set up to believe. He knows your background. He knows that your grandfather taught you the old ways."

She moved her head in one short nod. "He'll believe. He'll be just as big a sucker as I was." She raised her chin. "I'm going to call Rose and get her to bring him out. Now. Today."

When she turned toward the bathroom, he grabbed her arm, stopping her. "Listen to me. The boy needs real help. Not a charade born of revenge."

She shook off his arm and stepped away from him. "I told you once before, you're all I've got. You'll have to do."

TEN

Laken stood on the tarmac of a small airstrip near the national park. The plane she had chartered to bring Rosemary and C.J. from Allen was due any minute.

Marcus stood several feet away from her. She could feel his gaze on her, but she was doing her best to ignore it, the way he had so effectively ignored her in the past.

"You're tense," he said, the words brusque.

After a moment she said, "C.J.'s never flown before. I didn't know it would make me this nervous. I wish I were with him. I know nothing will happen. It's a reputable charter service, the same one that flew me out. But if he's scared—" She broke off and bit her lip. "I should be with him."

"He has your friend with him."

Nodding, she raised a hand to shade her eyes as she searched the distance. "Rose is great with

C.J.," she conceded. "She'll start an argument or insult him or something to take his mind off anything . . . like funny noises in the engine."

"There won't be any funny noises. C.J. is probably having the time of his life. He sounds like the kind of boy who knows how to enjoy an adventure."

She smiled. "He does. He likes new things. He's probably driving the pilot crazy with questions. Distracting him. Making him forget to watch—"

She broke off when she spotted a small plane in the distance. In the half hour that they had been there, she had seen half a dozen small planes in the distance, but somehow she knew this was the one that held her brother.

After it had rolled to a stop fifty feet or so from where they stood, a man jumped down and folded down the steps for the passengers. Laken, already moving toward it, laughed when she heard C.J. and Rosemary arguing.

"You *will* let him carry you. Understand me, you little fruit loop? The man will carry you. Your legs are too wobbly. If you try doing this on your own, you'll trip on the steps and your sister's first sight of you will be your brains splattered all over the tarmac."

Laken laughed again and walked faster. But somehow Marcus got there ahead of her, moving people out of the way, pushing his way into the plane.

"Charles Johnson Murphy, I presume." He had scooped C.J. up in his arms and was already making his way back down the steps.

C.J. stared into his face. "Yo," he said, his voice soft with awe. "And you're my faithful Indian companion?"

"The one and only."

As they moved past her Laken made no move to greet her brother. She simply stood and watched the two of them together with a tight pain gripping her chest. Why did it hurt to see Marcus holding the brother she loved so much? Why did it feel so heartbreakingly poignant?

Rosemary clutched at her arm with urgent fingers. "My God, why didn't you tell me? This is the Iceman? The hunk of granite? This is the intractable bastard you chased all over Chicago?"

"Yes, yes, yes," Laken said, smiling. "That covers the last three questions. As for the first, I did tell you. Right after I met him I told you he was sexier than Mrs. Watkins."

"But . . . but . . ."

Rose was still stuttering when Laken left her to move toward the Jeep.

Marcus had booked two rooms at the little motel behind the trading post. Laken and Rosemary would share one. C.J. and Marcus would take the other so that they could get to know each other before the healing ceremony that would take place the next evening.

Marcus had also talked to Anson Mathias.

Without a murmur of protest, the team working the site had agreed to clear out and give them privacy.

During dinner, which they had in the back room of the trading post, Laken kept C.J. and Rose talking about what had been going on during the past few days, but when they had finished their meal, C.J. rested both forearms on the table and looked from his sister to the man he had just met.

"Why don't we do it now?" he asked. "Why do we have to hang around here?"

Marcus leaned back in his chair. "You need to rest up from the flight and give Mathias time to clear the site."

"Yeah, I guess so." C.J.'s lips curved in a wicked smile. "Why don't you tell me what it was like being stuck in the wilderness with my sister? This is the first time I've ever known her to go more than half a day without her hair dryer."

Laken reached over and cuffed him on the back of the head. "I'll have you know I was terrific. All that hidden pioneer spirit came rushing to the fore, and before I knew it, there I was, rubbing sticks together to make fires, building lean-tos with my bare hands, making barbecue sauce for all the fresh game I killed and cleaned."

When C.J. and Rose fell into raucous laughter, Laken turned her head and found Marcus watching her. She kept her features even, pretending the tension between them didn't exist. At the moment all she had to hold on to was pretense.

During dinner, she had watched as her brother fell under this man's spell. She had watched him hanging on to every word Marcus spoke.

What kind of magic did he use that instantly turned the Murphys of the world into slaves?

"What's the matter?"

Laken glanced up to find Rosemary watching her.

"You look pale," the blonde said. "Are you sure you're all right?"

"I'm fine. Maybe a little tired." She tried out a smile. "Becoming one with the earth takes a lot out of you."

She hadn't told Rose that the whole thing was a big joke, that the ceremony would be fake. All day she had been trying to put that fact out of her mind. C.J. was much too good at reading her.

Laken somehow managed to get through the rest of the evening, but when darkness fell, when activity around the motel ceased and Rosemary finally drifted off to sleep, Laken lay in bed staring at the layers of shadow on the ceiling.

It was well after midnight when she finally got up, pulled on her friend's cotton robe, and left the room, heading for the courtyard at the center of the motel. There were wooden benches there and a small garden.

She would sit for a while and do some deep breathing until she was relaxed enough to sleep.

Laken didn't see Marcus until it was too late. She had already stepped into the moonlight, and he was already watching her. If she turned back now, it would look as though she were afraid of him. Which, of course, was damn close to the truth.

As she drew near enough to see his features, she realized he wasn't surprised to see her, almost as though he had been waiting for her.

When she reached the bench where he sat, he met her eyes. "He trusts me," he said, his voice quiet.

"You don't sound too happy about that."

He drew in a slow breath. "If this is going to work, I have to have his trust. But you're right, I'm not happy about it. He's a good kid. I don't like lying to him."

Nodding in understanding, Laken sat down beside him. "Stop worrying. When he's better, when he knows that his illness is truly behind him, I'll tell him the truth."

For a while no one spoke, then without looking at her, he said, "I hurt you, didn't I?"

Laken shot a look of disbelief in his direction. "Did I hear the tiniest smidge of humanity in your voice? Regret, maybe?" Her chin came up abruptly. "Damn you, if it's pity—"

"No, not pity."

She hesitated then gave a little laugh. "I could

tell you it was a case of proximity, or I could say that since I'm not all that experienced in the sex department, I mistook lust for something else. But you know me. I never learned how to play those polite little games." She leaned back and glanced away from him as she scratched the tip of her nose. "I can't pretend it was something less than it was. I fell in love with you. That's the long and short of it."

Tilting her head back, she stared up at the wide, midnight-blue sky. "After I met you," she said slowly, "when I saw that getting your help wasn't a sure thing, I was scared, as scared as I was when Mama and Daddy died. I had to fight the fear, and believe me, it was a battle royal. But I won. I came out of it stronger, more determined than ever. I made a vow to myself that night. I would make you help my brother. Whatever I had to do, I would do it. It didn't matter. I would crawl through hell if that's what it took."

She clasped her hands together tightly to steady them. "So," she said after a moment, "I'm there. On my hands and knees in hell."

"Laken—"

"No, don't say anything." She rose to her feet and looked down at him. "There's no need for you to kick yourself for what happened. I'm the one who made the deal. That night in Chicago, I agreed to pay the price. And believe it or not, I still think it was worth it."

Without giving him a chance to reply, she turned and walked away.

Laken leaned against the Jeep next to Rosemary and looked out over the site. It had obviously been worked. A grid with string borders was neatly laid out on their right. But the people, the equipment and tents, were all gone, leaving behind an eerie, haunted atmosphere.

Several yards to the left of the Jeep was a small pile of wood. A ceremonial fire waiting to be lit.

"I don't get it," Rosemary said.

"You don't have to get it," Laken told her, shifting her position in a restless movement. "He knows what he's doing."

"The sweating thing, I've seen that in movies. But when they're through, he's going to carry C.J. a mile, most of it uphill, just so they can bond? Why don't they do like all the other men I know and sit in front of the television, scratching and belching while they watch five or six football games?"

When Laken didn't respond, the blonde glanced at her. "You're not worried?"

"He won't let anything happen to C.J."

Rosemary moved a few steps away and, without looking at her friend, said, "Something happened, didn't it? While you two were in the hills together."

"I'd rather not talk about it right now, Rose." She gave a little laugh. "You know me, I always bounce back. Give me a couple of months and I'll be my old self again. I'll let you in on all the gory details and we can spend some time trashing him and men in general." She bit her lip. "Right now I—"

"You don't have to explain," her friend said. "I know. God, do I know. Men are pigs."

The last bit of light was retreating from the landscape when the women saw them coming over the rise. Both wore jeans. Their chests and feet were bare. Marcus had carried her brother over a mile of broken rock in his bare feet. Was this a result of Joseph Two Trees' training? Had Marcus been taught to endure without feeling?

When they reached the pile of wood where the women waited, Marcus settled C.J. on the ground beside it and walked to the Jeep.

C.J. glanced up at Laken. "He wasn't even breathing hard," he said, his voice filled with admiration and awe.

Marcus returned with a canteen of water and handed it to the boy. "Now you can have that drink you've been whining about, squirt."

"I was whining?" C.J. said, one brow raised. "I don't think so. I asked about water because I was concerned for you, O aged one. I was afraid a little exercise would give you a heart attack."

Marcus chuckled. "If you had eaten one more

piece of cake at dinner, it might have done it. For a skinny kid, you're no lightweight."

Laken glanced from one to the other. "Did you argue the whole time you were out there?"

"That wasn't an argument," her brother denied. "It was more like a friendly debate. Right, Marcus?"

"Right." Marcus glanced around. It was completely dark now and already the sky was filled with stars. "I guess it's time. Laken, you sit on C.J.'s left. Rose, you take the other side. That should put us roughly at the four points of the compass."

As they took their places Marcus lit a match and touched it to the wood. It caught immediately and moments later was blazing steadily.

C.J. stared at the fire for a moment then glanced around. "Are we going to sing 'Kum Ba Ya' now?"

When Marcus turned his head toward Laken, one brow raised, she shrugged. "What can I say, same genes."

Although he smiled, she could feel the tension building in him. She desperately wished that there was something she could do to help. Not just for C.J. For Marcus as well.

But there was nothing for her to do except wait. It was all up to him now.

Marcus moved his shoulders, trying to ease the tension in his muscles. Dammit, he had to pull this off.

It was crazy how he had connected with this skinny kid from the first moment he saw him. He didn't know if it was emotional intuition or a protective instinct or simply that C.J. was part of Laken. He only knew this was the most important thing he would do in his life.

The boy needed a miracle, and all he had was a fake.

The instant the thought formed in his mind, Marcus pulled himself up straighter. He couldn't think that way. He had to pretend, even to himself, that this was real.

And then suddenly he remembered some words. Only a few, but maybe it would be enough.

Across the campfire, Laken watched as the light flickered across the hard lines of Marcus's face and the smooth width of his bare chest.

Reaching into a leather pouch, he pulled out a handful of some powdery substance and offered it up to the four winds. As the flames caught it sparks flew up in the air, adding a touch of mysticism to the tense atmosphere.

"*Ein mah-ri eh ah-whit-to nei kee-mah.*"

His voice was low and steady, his expression calm. Although Laken couldn't decipher the words, she understood that he was announcing his presence to the things of the earth, calling for their assistance.

After a while, when he had repeated the same words several times, Laken began to feel that something was wrong. There was a look in his eyes she had never seen before. Something that looked very much like fear.

Glancing around, she looked at the shadows beyond the fire but saw nothing. And then she knew. The fear wasn't of something in the shadows, but of something in Marcus himself. A part of him that he had been denying, that he had been hiding from, was suddenly coming to the surface.

The silent battle he was fighting brought a glaze of perspiration to his face and chest, and closing his eyes, he murmured, "*Nei mah-voon-et ein. Nei mah-nah-ich-cah ein.*"

Seconds later he drew in a deep breath, his whole body thrown back in the process, and when he opened his eyes again, he was a different man. He was the pagan prince, a hard, adult version of the wild boy she had seen in the photograph.

When he began chanting, there was supreme confidence in his voice. He was no longer a supplicant. He was in command, and he was throwing out a challenge to phantom adversaries.

There was no fear in his eyes now. As he fought something Laken couldn't see his tone was arrogant, like a king giving orders to a recalcitrant knight.

And then there was hesitation. Frowning, he turned his head to stare at Laken. "*Nei mah-ocu-ah? Ka.*" Then louder, "*Ka!*"

He looked away from her, raising his fists as he nodded toward C.J. "*Nei ner-tah-mar. Tosi-tao-yo.*"

He glanced back at Laken, and suddenly she was no longer sitting cross-legged on the ground. She didn't remember coming to her feet, but the fire was no longer in front of her. It was below.

There was no wind, and no crackling sounds from the burning wood, no smell of smoke in the air. It was as though she moved through a vacuum with the rest of the world projected on a screen around her.

Marcus was close to her now, staring into her eyes as he lifted his hands, palms out. Her hands raised as well. When her palms came to rest against his, she could feel the texture of his skin and knew he was solid. This was real.

She laughed in delight when sparks of light, flickering like tiny fireflies, outlined their united hands. It was joy, made visible, spreading outward from their palms.

Laken blinked, and in the next moment she was sitting in the same spot as before.

She glanced around in confusion, but everything was exactly the same. It was as though nothing had happened. As though none of them had seen.

Across the fire, Marcus was sitting cross-legged, swaying with his continuing chant.

Before Laken could even raise a quiet protest, C.J. stiffened beside her. "Something's happening," he said.

Her brother didn't sound like himself at all. There was no flippancy in his voice, no calm logic. Rather than analyzing an event the way he usually did, he was completely caught up in it.

With an awkward, abrupt movement, his head jerked to the side and he toppled over backward. Immediately, violent tremors took control of his body.

Fear closed her throat and Laken moved to get to her feet.

"*Stay still,*" Marcus ordered. "I don't want anyone to move yet."

The chanting began again.

Perspiration slid down Laken's face as she waited, her fingers clenched into fists.

And then, as quickly as they had appeared, the tremors left her brother's body and he went completely still.

"*To-quet,*" Marcus said. "It's over."

Laken was already scrambling toward her brother. On her knees beside him, she pulled his head up to cradle it against her chest.

"C.J. *C.J.*" She sent a frantic glance in Marcus's direction. "What's wrong with him? Why isn't he—"

She broke off when she felt him stir against her. He opened his eyes and drew in a slow breath. "It's over," he said, repeating Marcus's words.

Pushing away from her, C.J. slowly climbed to his feet. Laken felt Rose's hand grasping hers tightly as they both watched. He moved steadily. Not a shiver. Not a shake.

Laken and Rose were laughing and crying at the same time as they took turns hugging C.J.

Glancing up, Laken saw Marcus standing on the other side of the fire, silently watching them.

When he caught her gaze on him, he turned abruptly and moved into the shadows.

Marcus paced back and forth in front of the wooden bench. It was almost two in the morning, but he knew he wouldn't sleep. When the motel room started to close in on him, he had come out here to fight the thing that was trying to control him.

Thing? he thought with a derisive smile twisting his lips. He could at least give it a name. It wasn't love. The capacity to love had been wiped out of him years ago. Need? Yes, he needed her. He had come to need her the way he needed air to breath.

He had told her once to be careful what she

asked of the gods. He should have taken his own advice. Disgusted by the coldness of his affairs, he had wished for more. Well, he got his wish. Dear heaven, did he ever get it.

He drew in a shuddering breath, remembering the look on her face when he had ended it. He had hurt her deeply, but the damage was small compared with what it would be later. If he hadn't pushed her away, if he gave into his need for her, eventually she would see him for what he was. She would know that all he could do was take, that he had nothing to give in return.

He had had the dream again last night. He was twelve again, running down a dirt road, chasing a black car. No matter how fast he ran, he couldn't catch it. Fear gripped him with tight, relentless fingers as the car got farther and farther away.

Through the windows, he could see them all. His mother and father. Old Joe. They were driving away, leaving him behind. They saw him. They heard him screaming for them to wait for him. They knew he was there, but one by one, they each turned away from the sight of him.

Always before, in the dream, Marcus watched as the car disappeared from sight, leaving him alone on the dirt road, his heart pounding with fear.

But this time was different. Suddenly the car stopped. The passenger door opened and Laken stepped out. She raised her hand, smiling as she called, "You don't have to be afraid, Marcus. I'll wait for you to catch up."

Sweet Jesus, he couldn't even get away from her in his dreams.

Clenching his fists, he forcibly rejected the dream and all it might imply. He forced his mind back to the past, back to the lessons he learned from his grandfather. Protect the vulnerable parts, Old Joe had taught him. Don't let the world know they exist. It was the only way to outsmart the elements of destruction. The only way to survive.

Once again Laken found him in the courtyard. Tonight he wasn't sitting on the bench. He stood beside it, his head tilted back as though he were reading the stars.

When she drew nearer, he heard her footsteps and glanced up.

"I didn't have a chance earlier to thank you." She drew in a slow breath. "You did it. You really . . ."

The words died as she saw his expression. "Why do you look like that?"

He shook his head. "You act as though I walked on water or something. I fooled him, just the way we planned. His fictional demon was eradicated by a fictional shaman in a fictional healing ceremony. It happens every day at tent revivals all over the country. Believe you'll be healed and you'll be healed."

Laken took an awkward step back. The contemptuous words hit her like a slap in the face.

"No," she whispered, denying the words, denying the cynicism in his dark eyes. "No," she said again. "You're wrong. It was real. And the healing wasn't all that happened during that ceremony. Something—" She broke off and wiped her palms on the sides of her jeans. "Some part of me was freed from my body. And the same thing happened to you. Whatever it was—this part of me that pulled free of mortality—it went toward you. And something in you reached out for it. It wasn't a joining. They . . . we simply touched." She glanced at him. "Stop shaking your head. I tell you, it happened."

"You were caught up in the mood," he told her, his voice devoid of emotion. "The same thing that happens when a whole crowd sees a statue cry."

"An illusion? Mass hysteria? No . . . no, it wasn't—"

"It was fake, remember?" His lips curved in a smile that mocked. "We agreed I would put on a show, and that's exactly what I did. Evidently I was pretty good, if you imagined you saw our souls touch."

Her head came up sharply. "Why did you call it that? I never said anything about our souls. I said I didn't know what it was."

He frowned, then moved his shoulders in a careless shrug. "I was simply exaggerating to show you how ridiculous the whole thing is. I hate to spoil your fantasy, but nothing happened."

Studying his face, she searched for some sign of the truth, something that would let her know how he felt. But there was nothing. He had hidden everything.

"I guess you'll be glad to get your life back," he said, his tone polite.

"Selling spark plugs to farmers . . . going to garage sales with Rose . . . watching C.J. play basketball with his friends." She smiled. "Yes, I'll be happy to have that again."

He turned his head away from her, and after an awkward moment of silence Laken cleared her throat. "Is this what it's usually like when you give a woman the old heave-ho? Stiff, polite conversation, like being trapped with a stranger in an elevator that's stuck between floors."

He gave a short laugh. "No, this is definitely not what it's like. Nothing about you is like anyone I've ever known. At this point I usually pull out my checkbook."

"Even when it lasted only a couple of days?"

"Even then."

She reached up to scratch the tip of her nose, cutting her eyes toward him. "You're not pulling it out."

"No."

"Because I didn't earn it?"

"Don't be stupid." His voice was low and harsh. "This was different. You're different."

Not so different, she told herself with a wry smile. He was dumping her just as he had dumped all the other women before her.

She drew in a slow breath. "So what comes after the check? Do we shake hands like civilized folk and wish each other well?"

"No." He was staring at her, his gaze focused on her mouth. "We share one last kiss . . . for old times' sake."

"For old times' sake," she whispered.

The kiss was fevered, desperate, and she almost allowed herself to believe that he would miss her when she had gone.

Too soon, it was over. He pulled back a fraction of an inch and, still holding her, said, "You'd better get some sleep. It's been a long day."

When she started to move away, she found that the hem of her cotton shirt was caught between his fingers. While she watched he released her, slowly, as though it were an effort to make his fingers move.

And then, as she turned to walk away, she heard him whisper, "Have a nice life, Laken."

ELEVEN

Laken stood on the porch, one arm wrapped around a wooden column, her hip resting against the balustrade. A light breeze rustled through the trees, making her shiver. Although so far it had been a warm November, the evenings were getting chilly.

When Cerberus suddenly jumped out of the darkness to land beside her, she swore under her breath.

"You hairless horror," she murmured, reaching down to rub the cat's back. "You're a disgrace to the animal kingdom."

"As an insult, that was pretty feeble," C.J. scoffed. "In fact, I can't remember the last time I heard you threaten to turn him into a really ugly rug."

He let the screen door slam behind him and moved to join her at the rail. Even now, two months later, Laken still felt a sense of relief every time she saw him walk like a normal twelve-year-old.

"I'm trying to be more sensitive to his skin condition," she said. "It can't be fun having all the girl cats snicker at him behind his back." She moved to the other side of the column. "Finish studying for the history test?"

When he didn't answer, she turned her head and found him watching her. "What?" She gave a little laugh and pushed the curls off her forehead. "Why are you staring at me like that?"

"When are you going to do something about Marcus?"

Laken caught her breath sharply and turned her head away so he couldn't see her expression.

"Just exactly what do you expect me to do?" she asked, struggling to keep her voice even.

"I don't know." When she glanced at him, he shrugged. "You always think of some way to work out a problem. How come you've just given up on this one?"

She exhaled a slow breath, intending her next words to be a sugarcoated explanation of male–female relations. But then she remembered who she was talking to.

Tilting her head back, she gave a weak laugh. "Maybe because our noble warrior gave me a very suave, very sophisticated kiss-off. I told you what happened."

"You told me what he told you, that the whole

thing was a hoax and the only reason he showed up for the actual healing was because you insisted. He said he didn't care about you and was only trying to get revenge for the way you bugged him in Chicago. Well, I don't buy it."

He moved around to the other side of her so he could see her face. "Know what I think? I think he was doing one of those twisted adult things. Like when there's only one piece of cake and all the adults say, 'No, no, I really don't care for cake,' when they really want to grab it and shove the whole thing in their mouth."

She made a choking sound. "I don't think I care for your analogy."

"Is that why you're turning red? Interesting. I didn't know you could still blush."

"You deviant little twit, just leave me alone. You weren't there. You didn't hear—"

"I heard him the night of the healing ritual. I saw how he looked at you." He paused. "I've done some research into the Comanche language. He called me his little white brother. Know what he called you?"

"He talked about me? You mean when he was fighting those things up in the hills?" She cut her eyes toward him. "You're making this up. You couldn't possibly know what he said. There were too many words."

"You know very well that I have perfect recall, and the language isn't that difficult once you figure out the sounds."

She frowned. "Why would he talk about me?"

He shrugged. "I got only one side of the conversation, so I don't know what started it all. It was about the time he started looking like a Norse god calling out the thunderbolts."

"A pagan prince," she corrected. "Yes, I remember. What did he call me?"

"He called you his woman. Not the woman. He said *my* woman."

The words brought a little twitch in her lower lip, but she kept her features even. "That doesn't mean anything. He was probably trying to fake out those . . . those invisible things."

"It wasn't a time for faking." C.J. put his hand on her shoulder. "Lake, I know this sounds weird, but the thing is, I felt something that night. Now it's two months later and I still feel it. Marcus belongs to us. And we belong to him."

Laken didn't ask him to elaborate, nor did she tell him he was imagining the whole thing. How could she when she knew exactly what he was talking about? She felt the same thing.

A moment later she sighed and leaned her cheek against the cold column. "He says nothing happened, C.J.," she whispered. "What if he's right and we're wrong?"

"We're not wrong. I don't know why he's lying. All I know is nothing will ever happen unless you stop being scared and go get him."

"Scared? I'm not—"

"Yes, you are."

She scratched the end of her nose with one finger. "Yes, I am," she admitted softly. "I'm scared to death. I don't think I could stand it if—"

"If you start thinking about a bunch of what ifs, nothing will ever get done. You have to make stuff happen, like you did in Chicago. You can do it, Lake."

She drew in a slow shaky breath. "When you're right, you're right." She pushed away from the column. "Okay, I guess I'll go get him."

The Comanche settlement was ten miles to the east of DeWitt, and on the day Laken first saw it, it was cold. Wind swept across the bare land in dry, frigid gusts and down the bare dirt streets.

Apparently the cold didn't affect the people who lived here, because she passed several construction sites where the men worked without coats or hats.

As she pulled up next to one of the sites, she remembered the conversation she had had two days earlier with Tess Defasio.

"The whole thing was weird," the brunette had told her. "On the surface he seemed the same, but something was definitely going on."

"What? What was different?"

"I can't really . . . well, like when he talked

to me. The words were pretty much the same, but it was like he was talking to a real person instead of a machine who kept track of his appointments. To tell you the truth, it made me kind of sad. Like a statue had come to life and was trying to learn how to deal with being flesh and blood. After a week he stopped by my desk to tell me he was taking an extended leave of absence and—" She broke off and cleared her throat. "Laken, he thanked me for putting up with him and being such a loyal employee. God, I almost broke down and cried right in front of him."

"But he didn't say where he was going?"

"Not to me. He just said he didn't know when he'd be back."

And according to his aunt Miriam, Marcus had also kept his family in the dark.

"I don't know where he is or what he's doing." The older woman's voice was laced with acid. "But I want you to know I hold you responsible for everything. We've had nothing but misery since the day you turned up."

Five minutes after Miriam hung up on Laken, Philip called.

"Miriam doesn't know I'm calling," he told her, "so I have to talk fast. I felt it was my duty to tell you that she wasn't being quite honest with you, my dear. The fact is, Marcus came to us and told us where he was going. And he said he was almost certain he wouldn't be back." He paused.

"Please don't think too badly of my wife. She loves Marcus. Unfortunately love is an emotion she's never learned to deal with."

"I don't blame her." Her fingers tightened on the receiver. "Where is he, Philip?"

"He went to the Comanche settlement near DeWitt."

And now Laken was there as well.

As soon as she stepped from her car, a stocky man who had the look of Joseph Two Trees approached her.

"Can I help you?"

She smiled. "I hope so. I'm looking for Marcus Reed."

When he raised his head, staring at something beyond her, Laken swung around. Marcus, wearing jeans and flannel shirt like the other men, was moving toward her.

He had changed. He was thinner and the lines of his face were sharper.

"Ralph," he said as he reached them, "I'd like you to meet Laken Murphy. Laken, this is my cousin, Ralph White Deer."

After returning the other man's greeting, Laken glanced at Marcus. "I need to talk to you."

Ralph glanced at Marcus, who gave a barely perceptible nod, then said, "I guess I'd better get back before Hector decides to try that electric saw again. It was nice meeting you, Laken."

As soon as he had moved away, Laken said, "Is there somewhere we can go that's less public?" She glanced toward the row of houses on the other side of the street. "I don't want to sound paranoid, but I think we're being watched."

"They're good people, but they tend to be overprotective."

She raised one arched brow. "They think you need protecting from me?"

He shrugged. "You're an outsider. They don't know what's in your heart."

"Do you?"

Without answering, he began to walk. Laken followed as he led her between two houses and onto the open plain.

"Will this do?" he asked when they were a hundred yards or so from the nearest house.

Laken nodded. Now that she was here, now that she had finally found him, she couldn't think what to do next. She couldn't exactly say, "Pack your things, I'm taking you home with me."

She cleared her throat. "Could you— I was wondering why you left Chicago. Of course, you don't have to tell me. I mean, if it's too personal or anything."

He turned his eyes toward the horizon and the silence stretched out.

"When Aunt Miriam took me to Chicago," he said finally, "she and Philip did their best to make me feel a part of their world. They encouraged me to forget the first twelve years of my life. And after a while it worked. I forgot. At least I thought I had." He paused, still not looking at her. "Then you came along. You forced me to remember. And in recalling the past, I had to acknowledge how pointless my life in Chicago was."

"So you came here."

"So I came here. I couldn't be the man my aunt wanted me to be, so I came here to be the man Joseph Two Trees wanted me to be." He gave a short, harsh laugh. "And found out I can't be that either."

There was something in his voice, something she didn't recognize. Before she could pin it down, he was talking again, and his voice was back to normal.

"Even though I'm not going to stay here, I've worked up a plan for inexpensive housing that will keep the Comanche traditions alive while giving them decent places to live. As you saw, they're doing the building themselves." He paused. "They have a tremendous amount of pride. It would be easier on them if they lived on a reservation, but that's not what they want. They need to be independent. Because I'm one of them, at least technically, they're letting me provide the materials."

Technically. He was hiding his disappointment, the way he tried to hide everything, but Laken knew him as no one else ever had.

"Strange," she said, her voice quiet. "It's your vision, isn't it?"

He glanced at her. "My vision?"

"What's happening back there." She waved a hand toward the settlement. "You're fulfilling your destiny. You're of the Comanche, but not with them. You're working to unite the past and present and bring that union into the light."

She paused, rubbing her palms on the sides of her jeans. "I've been thinking about it and it seems to me your vision was also telling you that you are first and foremost an individual. You're Marcus Aurelius Starwalker Reed, a man who belongs to himself."

She drew in a slow breath, gathering her courage. "And to me."

His face turned hard and he glanced away from her.

"You can deny it until you run out of breath, but it won't change anything," she said, her voice firm. "You know it. I know it. Even C.J. knows it. Our souls touched, Marcus. That means something. That *means* something."

Marcus just wanted her to stop talking and go away. He had it all worked out until she showed up. She was screwing up everything.

He had intentionally put how much he needed her out of his mind. He had to make her go away before the need took over again.

"Maybe you're right," he said finally. "I suppose it's possible that something happened that night."

He saw hope in her eyes and deliberately determined to smash it. "But what you're not taking into consideration," he continued slowly, "is the fact that I have a free will. I'm not bound by the mystical. I can accept or reject, as I choose." He paused. "I reject."

With that, he turned and walked away.

Before he had turned back into the stone-faced automaton, Laken had seen what was in his deep-set black eyes. The same thing that she had seen in his childhood photo. Savage, unendurable pain. He was an injured animal, turning on her because she dared to get close.

But Laken had a free will as well. And she'd be damned if she'd let him do this.

"You're lonely, Marcus," she called to him. "Admit it. You're a lonely man."

He shrugged and said, "So?"

"So why are you determined to stay that way? For thirty-seven years, loneliness has been your constant companion. You don't have to worry about it ever leaving you. Loneliness is nothing if not faithful. It's always there for you."

His long strides were taking him farther away from her. She had to stop him.

"I want to make a deal," she said, raising her voice.

He stopped. He didn't say anything, he didn't even turn to look at her, but at least he stopped.

"Let me take its place for a while." The words ran into one another. She knew she had to talk fast, she had to make him hear her before he started walking again. "It'll just be a trial run. You know, to see how it works out."

He glanced over his shoulder with a frown. "What are you talking about?"

"It's simple. For the next thirty-seven years of your life, instead of loneliness, I'll be your constant companion."

His features grew hard again. "I'm not in the mood for games."

She moved a step closer. "It's not a game. It's a genuine offer. You should think it over, Marcus. You won't get better terms anywhere else. And it's not like you would be making a commitment or anything. You can leave all your hidden things hidden and give only the parts you feel comfortable giving. A little companionship. A little sex. A tango now and then. What could it hurt?" Her lips curved in an unsteady smile. "See? I'm not really a threat to you. Just an ordinary working girl. A man like you—wealthy, powerful, educated, and upper-crust—why you can outthink me a hundred times over."

He gave a short, harsh laugh. "That's a load of crap and you know it. All you have to do is look at me and—"

He broke off abruptly, as though he had suddenly realized that his guard was slipping, and began to walk again.

Laken stumbled to catch up with him. Fear was squeezing the breath out of her, constricting her heart.

"Don't walk away from me!" she screamed at his back. "You coward! You—you—"

When he reached a small rise, he stopped and turned slightly, so that she saw his face in profile. He was the warrior again. He needed no one. And nothing she could say would make a difference.

She had lost. Pain diminished her, as though her own body were caving in on itself.

Marcus stared straight ahead at the never-ending plain. Strange that it wasn't all that hard to walk away from her. Just shut everything off and walk away. He was back in familiar territory now, where nothing counted, nothing mattered. Nothing hurt.

When he heard her shouting at him, he turned to look at her.

"Go ahead," she called. "Be above mortal and see what it gets you. You won't ever have any problems. You'll have *nothing!* You hear?"

She took another step toward him. "No matter what you said, no matter what the civilized part of you wants to believe, in your heart you know you healed C.J. It was real. The curse was real and so was the healing ceremony. So I have another one for you. I'm putting a curse on you, Marcus. I don't have any herbs to fling around or spirits to summon forth, but I guarantee it will work."

She paused to draw in a deep, trembling breath. "On this day of November the tenth, I, Laken Pegeen Murphy, being of sound mind, hereby assign to Marcus Aurelius Starwalker Reed, the curse of eternal coldness.

"In your heart it will be forever November. For the rest of your life, you'll be alone. No warmth for you, Marcus. No children or grandchildren to cuddle on your lap and warm you in your old age. No one to hold your hand when you lie dying."

Her voice was broken, her face ravaged. When he saw what he was doing to her, Marcus took a step toward her, then stopped himself. No one could love him like that. It was a passing thing. She would get over it soon enough.

When she spoke again, her voice was barely audible. "When I first knew I loved you, the joy was so incredibly intense, it felt like pain. It was like nothing I ever felt before. Have you? Have you ever felt happiness so overwhelming it hurt? Right then, right at that moment, it didn't matter whether or not you loved me back. The act of loving was the thing. I loved. Do you understand? I *loved.*"

She wiped the tears from her cheeks with shaking fingers. "Since then, I've felt a lot of pain." She gave a short laugh. "But not the kind inspired by joy. Your coldness hurt. Being unable to reach you hurt. And I felt a special kind of pain in knowing that you hadn't felt that moment of incredible happiness the way I did. I wished that for you. Knowing you wouldn't ever feel hurt like hell. And right now . . . right now I'm being ripped apart by pain because I can't make you stay. But you know what? All the pain I've felt since then can't take away that first moment of joy."

She was crying so hard now that she could barely speak. "Now I'm glad you didn't get any of the joy. And you never will because of my curse. You're stupid and stiff-necked and cowardly. You're hateful. A cold, hateful bastard. You don't deserve . . . you don't deserve to—"

Breaking off, she stooped down and grabbed a clump of dried dirt and threw it. When it hit him in the shoulder, he began moving toward her, dodging as she threw another and another.

Reaching her in a few strides, he grabbed her shoulders and gave her a hard shake. "Stop it. Laken . . . Laken, stop it."

When she raised her head to look at him, the naked pain and undiminished love brought a groan from deep in his chest and he clasped her hard against him.

"You're so damned stubborn." He pulled a handkerchief out of his pocket and shoved it into her hand. "Here, blow your nose."

She obediently wiped her eyes and blew her nose. "What kind of warrior carries a linen hanky?" she muttered.

Placing a hand on either side of her face, he stared into her eyes. "This is impossible. Can't you see that?"

"A thing's only impossible until somebody does it."

He groaned again. "You have no idea what you're doing. You've built up some naive picture of us living happily ever after. If you knew—Laken, it's not just that I don't fit in here or Chicago. My whole life, my whole existence is fake. Do away with the fake part and there's nothing left. A black hole. That's what I am. Do you understand? I've looked inside, below the pretense, and there was nothing. My God, a woman like you—" He broke off and swallowed hard. "You're real. I've never met anyone as real as you. You deserve so much more."

"You're kidding," she said, genuinely shocked. "You can't really believe that. That you're nothing more than a collection of false identities. Do you know how many people care about you? I talked to a lot of them this week. And it's not Marcus Reed, hotshot architect, they care about. Or Mark Starwalker. It's you." She tapped his chest for emphasis. "These were good, decent people. Smart people. Tess. Miriam and Philip. Leon. Mrs. Curtis. And C.J. Don't tell me you could pull a fast one on my brother, because I won't believe it. That kid can spot a fake a mile off. And he told me to come get you and bring you home."

For one brief moment Marcus almost let himself believe. "You're crazy to be here. And I'm crazy for listening to you. Why in hell didn't you just let me leave?" he muttered. "Why in hell can't I look at this face without wanting to kiss it?"

"Because I'm just so damn adorable you can't resist? Because you're hot to get me back in bed? Because you know you'll die if you leave me?" she said in a hoarse whisper. "Choose one."

"All of the above," he groaned as his lips found hers.

Later, a good while later, he drew in a shuddering breath. "Take the curse off," he ordered.

"Lifting curses isn't that easy. It's not like I can just snap my fingers and it's gone. There are things that have to come first. You have to promise you'll never—" She broke off and steadied her trembling lips. "You have to promise you'll never walk away from me again."

"Never," he whispered.

"You said that too quickly. Think about it. You have to understand what you're promising.

When you swear not to walk away, that means you have to stay with me for the rest of your life."

He hesitated, then said, "For as long as you want me."

"That will be for the rest of my life," she whispered. "By the power vested in me, I hereby declare Marcus Aurelius Starwalker Reed curse free."

She paused, studying his face, her eyes filled with warmth and love, indulgent, as though he were a recalcitrant child.

"Still don't quite believe, do you? You still think this will end in pain."

He didn't believe. But it didn't matter anymore. He could hurt himself, but he couldn't stand hurting her. He would stay with her as long as she would let him.

"I want to be with you, Laken. Whatever that means, whatever it costs, I want to stay with you." He drew in a slow breath, then he said the words. "I need you, Laken."

When she smiled up at him, he realized it was a pretty weak declaration. If they were to have any chance at all, there had to be truth between them, but dear God, she deserved so much more.

"I wish I could say . . . I wish I could believe . . ."

Smiling, she laid a finger against his lips, stopping the words. "Don't worry about it. We're in no hurry. I'll wait for you to catch up."

Marcus felt the words, an echo of his dream,

wash over him, weakening him. As he held her tightly against him something warm and bright entered his closed-off world.

If he hadn't known better, he would have sworn it was love.

THE EDITOR'S CORNER

It's a magical time of year, with ghosts and goblins, haunted houses and trick-or-treating. What better way to indulge yourself than with our four enchanting romances coming next month! These sexy, mystical men offer our heroines their own unique blend of passion and love. Truly, you are going to be LOVESWEPT by these stories that are guaranteed to heat your blood and keep you warm through the chilly days ahead.

The wonderfully unique Ruth Owen starts off our lineup with **SORCERER**, LOVESWEPT #714. Jillian Polanski has always been able to hold her own with Ian Sinclair, but when they enter the machine he's created to explore an unreal world, she becomes his damsel in distress and he the knight who'll risk his life to save hers. In this magic realm Ian's embrace stirs buried longings and dangerous desires, but now she must trust this dark lord with her dreams. Once again Ruth will draw you into a breathtaking adventure that is both playful and heartbreaking.

Marcia Evanick's hero walks right **OUT OF A DREAM,** LOVESWEPT #715! With a mysterious crash Clayton Williams appears in Alice Jorgensen's parlor on Halloween night—and convinces the lady in the rabbit suit that he'll be nothing but trouble. Unwilling to let her escape his passionate pursuit, Clayton insists on moving into her boardinghouse and vows to learn her secrets. Can she risk loving a daredevil with stars in his eyes? Marcia weaves bewitching magic and celebrates the delightful mystery of true love.

Jan Hudson is on a **HOT STREAK,** LOVESWEPT #716, with a hero who sizzles. Amy Jordan wonders how an out-of-this-world gorgeous man could look so heartbroken, then races out into the rain to rescue him! After disaster struck his research, Dr. Neil Larkin felt shattered . . . but once Amy ignites a flame of hope with kisses that would melt holes in a lab beaker, he is enchanted—struck by the lightning of steamy, sultry attraction no science could explain. Jan does it again with this touching and funny story that makes for irresistible reading.

Last but never least is **IMAGINARY LOVER,** LOVESWEPT #717, by the ever popular Sandra Chastain. Dusty O'Brian can't believe her aunt has left the old house to her and to Dr. Nick Elliott! The pain burning in the doctor's mesmerizing dark eyes echoes her own grief, but she's been pushing people away for too long to reach out to him—and he needs her too fiercely to confess his hunger. Is she his forbidden desire sent by fate, or the only woman who can make him whole? Sandra evokes this romantic fantasy with stunning power and unforgettable passion.

Happy reading!

With warmest wishes,

Beth de Guzman

Senior Editor

P.S. Don't miss the women's novels coming your way in November: **PURE SIN,** from the award-winning Susan Johnson, is a sensuous tale of thrilling seduction set in nineteenth-century Montana; **SCANDAL IN SILVER,** from bestselling author Sandra Chastain, is her second Once Upon a Time Romance and takes its cue from *Seven Brides for Seven Brothers;* **THE WINDFLOWER** is a beautifully written romance from the bestselling Sharon and Tom Curtis in which two worlds collide when an innocent lady is kidnapped by the pirate she has sworn to bring to justice. We'll be giving you a sneak peek at these wonderful books in next month's LOVESWEPTs. And immediately following this page, look for a preview of the terrific romances from Bantam that are *available now!*

TERESA MEDEIROS

THIEF OF HEARTS

"Ms. Medeiros casts a spell with her poignant writing."—*Rendezvous*

From the storm-lashed decks of a pirate schooner to the elegant grounds of an English estate comes a spellbinding tale of love and deception . . . as only the remarkable bestselling author Teresa Medeiros can tell it. . . .

"I've heard enough about your cowardly tactics, Captain Doom, to know that your favored opponents are helpless women and innocent children afraid of ghosts."

A loose plank creaked behind her, startling her. If he had touched her then, she feared she would have burst into tears.

But it was only the mocking whisper of his breath that stirred her hair. "And which are you, Miss Snow? Innocent? Helpless? Or both?" When his provocative question met with stony silence, he resumed his pacing. " 'Tis customary to scream and weep when one is abducted by brigands, yet you've done neither. Why is that?"

Lucy didn't care to admit that she was afraid he'd embroider a skull and crossbones on her lips. "If I might have gained anything by screaming, you'd have left me gagged, wouldn't you? It's obvious by the motion of the deck that the ship is at full sail, precluding immediate rescue. And I've never found tears to be of any practical use."

"How rare." The note in his voice might have been one of mockery or genuine admiration. "Logic and intelligence wrapped up in such a pretty package. Tell me, is your father in the habit of allowing you to journey alone on a navy frigate? Young ladies of quality do not travel such a distance unchaperoned. Does he care so little for your reputation?

Lucy almost blurted out that her father cared for nothing *but* her reputation, but to reveal such a painful truth to this probing stranger would have been like laying an old wound bare.

"The captain's mother was traveling with us." Fat lot of good that had done her, Lucy thought. The senile old woman had probably slept through the attack. "The captain of the *Tiberius* is a dear friend of my father's. He's known me since I was a child. I can promise you that should any of the men under his command so much as smile at me in what might be deemed an improper manner, he'd have them flogged."

"Purely for your entertainment, I'm sure."

Lucy winced at the unfair cut. "I fear my tastes in amusement don't run to torture, as yours are rumored to," she replied sweetly.

"Touché, Miss Snow. Perhaps you're not so helpless after all. If we could only ascertain your innocence with such flair . . ."

He let the unspoken threat dangle, and Lucy swallowed a retort. She couldn't seem to stop her tart tongue from running rampant. She'd do well to remember that this man held both her life and her virtue captive in his fickle hands.

His brisk footsteps circled her, weaving a dizzying

spell as she struggled to follow his voice. "Perhaps you'd care to explain why your noble papa deprived himself of your charming wit for the duration of your voyage."

"Father took ill before we could leave Cornwall. A stomach grippe. He saw no logic in my forfeiting my passage, but feared travel by sea would only worsen his condition."

"How perceptive of him. It might even have proved fatal." He circled her again. His footsteps ceased just behind her. Doom's clipped tones softened. "So he sent you in his stead. Poor, sweet Lucy."

Lucy wasn't sure what jarred her most—the rueful note of empathy in his voice or hearing her Christian name caressed by his devilish tongue. "If you're going to murder me, do get on with it," she snapped. "You can eulogize me *after* I'm gone."

The chair vibrated as he closed his hands over its back. Lucy started as if he'd curled them around her bare throat. "Is that what they say about me, Miss Snow? That I'm a murderer?"

She pressed her eyes shut beneath the blindfold, beset by a curious mix of dread and anticipation. "Among other things."

"Such as?"

"A ghost," she whispered.

He leaned over her shoulder from behind and pressed his cheek to hers. The prickly softness of his beard chafed her tender skin. His masculine scent permeated her senses. "What say you, Lucy Snow? Am I spirit or man?"

There was nothing spectral about his touch. Its blatant virility set Lucy's raw nerves humming. She'd never been touched with such matter-of-fact intimacy by anyone.

The odd little catch in her breath ruined her prim reply. "I sense very little of the spiritual about you, sir."

"And much of the carnal, no doubt."

His hand threaded through the fragile shield of her hair to find her neck. His warm fingers gently rubbed her nape as if to soothe away all of her fears and melt her defenses, leaving her totally vulnerable to him. Lucy shuddered, shaken by his tenderness, intrigued by his boldness, intoxicated by his brandy-heated breath against her ear.

"Tell me more of the nefarious doings of Captain Doom," he coaxed.

She drew in a shaky breath, fighting for any semblance of the steely poise she had always prided herself on. "They say you can skewer your enemies with a single glance."

"Quite flattering, but I fear I have to use more conventional means." His probing fingertips cut a tingling swath through the sensitive skin behind her ears. "Do go on."

Lucy's honesty betrayed her. "They say you've been known to ravish ten virgins in one night." As soon as the words were out, she cringed, wondering what had possessed her to confess such a shocking thing.

Instead of laughing, as she expected, he framed her delicate jaw in his splayed fingers and tilted her head back.

His voice was both tender and solemn, mocking them both. "Ah, but then one scrawny virgin such as yourself would only whet my appetite."

"They also swear you won't abide babbling," Lucy blurted out, knowing she was doing just that.

"That you'll sew up the lips of anyone who dares to defy you."

His breath grazed her lips. "What a waste that would be in your case. Especially when I can think of far more pleasurable ways to silence them."

Courting Miss Hattie
BY
Pamela Morsi

The nationally bestselling author of WILD OATS

"A refreshing new voice in romance."
—Jude Deveraux

Award-winning author Pamela Morsi has won readers' hearts with her unforgettable novels—filled with romance, humor, and her trademark down-to-earth charm. And with her classic COURTING MISS HATTIE, Morsi pairs an unlikely bride and an irresistible suitor who learn that love can be found in the most unexpected places.

"All right, explain to me about kissing."

"There are three kinds of kisses."

"Right," she said skeptically. "Don't tell me, they're called hook, line, and sinker."

"That's fishing. This is kissing. I know a lot about both, and if you want to know what I know, listen up and mind your manners."

He'd released her hands, and she folded them primly in her lap, sitting up straight like a good pupil. Her expression was still patently skeptical, though. "Okay, three kinds of kisses," she repeated, as if trying to remember.

"There's the peck, the peach, and the malvalva."

Hattie didn't bother to control her giggle. "The mal-whata?"

"Malvalva. But we haven't got to that one yet."

"And with luck, we never will. This is pure silliness," she declared.

"You admitted yourself that you know nothing about kissing," Reed said. "It's easy, but you've got to learn the basics."

"I'm all ears."

"Ears are good, but I think we ought to start with lips."

"Reed!"

There was laughter in his eyes as a flush colored her face, but he continued his discourse matter-of-factly, as if he were explaining a new farming method. "Okay, the peck is the most common kiss. It's the kind you're already familiar with. That's what you gave your folks and such. You just purse your lips together and make a little pop sound, like this." He demonstrated several times, his lips pursing together seductively, then releasing a little kiss to the air.

Hattie found the sight strangely titillating. "Okay, I see what you mean," she said.

"Show me," he instructed.

She made several kisses in the air while Reed inspected her style. "I feel like an idiot!" she exclaimed after a moment. "I must look so silly."

"Well," he admitted, "kissing the air is a little silly. But when it's against your sweetheart's lips, it doesn't feel silly at all."

She made several more self-conscious attempts as he watched her lips. "Is this the way?" she asked.

"I think you'll do fine with that." He shifted his position a bit and looked past her for a moment. "That's a good first kiss for someone like Drayton," he said seriously, then grinned. "Don't let him get the good stuff until later."

She opened her mouth to protest, but he cut her short. "Now, the second kind of kiss is called a peach. It's a bit different from the peck." He reached out and grasped her shoulders, scooting her a little closer. "This is the one that lovers use a lot."

"Why do they call it a peach?" she asked curiously.

His smile was warm and lazy. " 'Cause it's so sweet and juicy."

"Juicy?" she repeated worriedly.

"Just a little. First, open your mouth a little, about this wide." He demonstrated.

"Open my mouth?"

"Yes, just a little. So you can taste the other person."

"Taste?"

"Just a little. Try it."

She held her lips open as he'd shown her. He nodded encouragement. "That's about right," he said. "Now you need to suck a bit."

"Suck?"

"Just a bit."

She shook her head, waving away the whole suggestion. "This is ridiculous, Reed. I can't do it."

He slid closer to her. "It only feels ridiculous because you're doing it without a partner. Here . . ." He again grasped her shoulders and pulled her near. "Try it on me. You won't feel nearly as silly, and it'll give you some practice."

"You want me to kiss you?"

"Just for practice. Open your mouth again."

She did as she was told, her eyes wide in surprise. Reed lowered his head toward hers, his lips also parted invitingly. "When I get close like this," he said, his breath warm on her cheek, "you turn your head a little."

"Why?"

"So we won't bump noses."

Following his lead, she angled her head. "That's right. Perfect," he whispered the instant before his lips touched hers.

It was a gentle touch, and only a touch, before he moved back slightly. "Don't forget to suck," he murmured.

"Suck."

"Like a peach."

"Like a peach."

Then his mouth was on hers again. She felt the tenderness of his lips and the insistent pressure of the vacuum they created. She did as he'd instructed, her mouth gently pulling at his. A little angle, a little suction, a little juicy, and very, very warm.

"What do you think?" he whispered against her mouth.

"Nice" was all she got out before he continued his instruction.

They pulled apart finally, and Hattie opened her eyes in wonder. The blood was pounding in her veins. Staring at Reed, she saw mirrored on his face the same pleased confusion she felt. "I did it right?" she asked, but she knew the answer already. Kissing might be new to her, but it was impossible not to believe that what she felt was exactly why courting couples were always looking for a moment of privacy.

"Yes," Reed answered. He slid his arms around her back and pulled her more firmly against his chest. "Do you think you can do it again?"

VIRGIN BRIDE
BY
TAMARA LEIGH

"Fresh, exciting . . . wonderfully sensual . . . sure to be noticed in the romance genre."
—Amanda Quick

Tamara Leigh burst onto the romance scene with WARRIOR BRIDE and was praised by authors and critics alike. Now with VIRGIN BRIDE she offers another electrifying tale of a woman who would give anything to avoid being sent to a convent—even her virtue.

"Enough!" The anguished cry wrenched itself from Graeye's throat. All her life she had been looked upon with suspicion, but now, with her world crashing down around her, she simply could take no more accusations—and most especially from this man . . . a man to whom she had given her most precious possession.

Driven by renewed anger, she was unable to check the reckless impulse to wipe the derision from Balmaine's face. She raised her arm and a moment later was amazed at the ease with which she landed her palm to his face. With the exception of William, never before had she struck another.

"I am but a human being cursed to bear a mark set upon my face—not by the devil but by God." In her tirade she paid no heed to the spreading red left by her hand, or the sparkle of fury that leaped to Balmaine's eyes.

" 'Tis a mark of birth, naught else," she continued. "You have nothing to fear from me that you would not fear from another."

"So the little one has claws, eh?" He made the observation between clenched teeth. " 'Tis as I thought."

One moment Graeye was upright, face-to-face with this hard, angry man, and the next she was on her back, that same face above hers as those spectacular orbs bored into her.

"Had I the time or inclination," he said, "I might be tempted to tame that terrible temper of yours. But as I've neither, you will have to content yourself with this."

Temper? But she didn't—Graeye had no time to ponder his estimation of her nature before she felt his mouth on hers. The thought to resist never entered her mind.

When he urged her to open to him, she parted her lips with a sigh and took him inside. Slowly his tongue began an exploration of the sensitive places within—places he knew better than she.

Turning away from the insistent voices that urged her to exercise caution, she welcomed the invasion and recklessly wound her arms around him, pressing herself to his hard curves. When his hand slid between them to stroke that place below her belly, she arched against it.

Then, as abruptly as it had begun, it was over, and she was left to stare up at the man who had so effortlessly disengaged himself from her.

In the blink of an eye he had turned from passionate lover to cold and distant adversary. How was it he had such control over his emotions when she had none? Was she too long suppressed?

"I may have fallen prey to your wiles last eventide," he said, smoothing his hands down his tunic. "But I assure you I have no intention of paying the price you would ask for such an unfortunate tryst. Your scheme has failed, Lady Graeye."

To gather her wits about her after such a thorough attack upon her traitorous senses was not an easy thing, but the impact of his words made it less difficult than it would otherwise have been. Doing her utmost to put behind what had just occurred, she lifted herself from the bench and stood before him.

"You err," she said in a terribly small voice that made her wince. Drawing a deep breath, she delivered her next words with more assurance. "There is naught I want from you that you have not already given."

His eyes narrowed. "And what do you think you have stolen from me?"

She lifted her chin a notch, refusing to be drawn into a futile argument as to whether she had stolen or been given his caresses.

"Though you do not believe me," she said, "I tell you true that I did not know who you were until this morn. 'Twas freedom from the Church I hoped to gain, not a husband—that is what you gave me."

Nostrils flaring, Balmaine gave a short bark of laughter. "Be assured, Lady Graeye," he said as he adjusted his sword on its belt, "you will return to the abbey. Though you are no longer pure enough to become a nun, there will be a place for you there at the convent. You will go . . . even if I have to drag you there myself."

The convent . . . She took a step nearer him. " 'Tis not your decision whether—"

His hand sliced impatiently through the air. "Ultimately *everything* that has anything to do with Medland is under my control. You had best accept it and resign yourself to entering the convent."

Her heart began to hammer against her ribs. Was what he said true? Could he, in fact, usurp her father's rights over her? If so, since he was determined to return her to Arlecy, all would have been for naught. Biting her lip, she bowed her head and focused upon the hilt of his sword.

"Then I would ask you to reconsider, Baron Balmaine, and allow me to remain with my father. He is not well and is in need of someone—"

"The decision has been made," he interrupted again, then turned on his heel and strode away.

Even if Graeye could have contained the anger flaring through her, she would not have. There was nothing left to lose. "You have a rather nasty penchant for rudely interrupting when one is trying to speak," she snapped. " 'Tis something you really ought to work at correcting."

Seething, she stared at his back, willing him to turn again.

He did not disappoint her, returning to tower over her and looking every bit the barbarian. "In future, if you have anything to say to me, Lady Graeye, I would prefer you address my face rather than my back. Do you understand?"

Though she knew he could easily crush her between his hands if he so desired—and at that moment he certainly looked tempted to—Graeye managed to quell the instinct to cower. After all, considering the fate that awaited her, it hardly mattered what he might do. She gathered the last shreds of her courage about her and drew herself up, utilizing every hair's breadth of height she had.

"In future, you say?" She gave a short, bitter laugh. "As we have no future together, Baron, 'tis an entirely absurd request. Or should I say 'order'?"

His lids snapped down to narrow slits, a vein in his forehead leaping to life. "Sheathe your claws, little cat," he hissed, his clenched fists testament to the control he was exercising. "The day is still young and we have games yet to play."

Then he was walking away again, leaving her to stare after him with a face turned fearful.

And don't miss these sizzling romances from Bantam Books, on sale in October:

WANTED

by the nationally bestselling author

Patricia Potter

"One of the romance genre's finest talents."
—*Romantic Times*

SCANDAL IN SILVER

by the highly acclaimed

Sandra Chastain

"Sandra Chastain's characters' steamy relationships are the stuff dreams are made of."
—*Romantic Times*

THE WINDFLOWER

by the award-winning

Sharon & Tom Curtis

"Sharon and Tom's talent is immense."
—LaVyrle Spencer